BRAZEN

POWERTOOLS: THE SHIELDS, BOOK 3

JAYNE RYLON

HAPPY ENDINGS PUBLISHING

V4

eBook ISBN: 978-1-947093-28-7

Print ISBN: 978-1-947093-29-4

Cover Design by Jayne Rylon

Editing by Mackenzie Walton

Proofreading by Fedora Chen

Formatting by Jayne Rylon

ABOUT THE BOOK

They were sent to kill him, but fell in love with him instead.

Sola doubted her instincts after her best friend and partner on the Shields security team, Aarav, acted for months like the attraction between them didn't exist. One wild night on their boss's private jet proves she was spot on even if she has no idea where their relationship will go from there.

When they're sent to assassinate the head of a money laundering operation at a brand new casino, Sola looks into the eyes of their target and her gut screams he's not the source of the evil they're hunting. Risking everything, Sola steps in between the man she loves and the one they've been sent to kill.

Her instant and undeniable attraction to their unintended captive forces them to investigate him further and decide

—will they eliminate him, protect him, or entice him to join their intimate partnership?

Brazen is a bisexual multipartner romance in NYT and USA Today bestselling author Jayne Rylon's fan-favorite Powertools Universe. Visit your favorite characters or meet new ones in this interconnected, why choose standalone in the Powertools: The Shields MMF ménage series.

ADDITIONAL INFORMATION

Sign up for the Naughty News for contests, release updates, news, appearance information, sneak peek excerpts, reading-themed apparel deals, and more. www. jaynerylon.com/newsletter

Shop for autographed books, reading-themed apparel, goodies, and more www.jaynerylon.com/shop

A complete list of Jayne's books can be found at www. jaynerylon.com/books

1

—————

Aarav dashed across the roof of the Shields' headquarters toward the sleek black chopper that touched down on the building's helipad. Through the bubble of tinted windshield, he recognized the pilot who most often flew his boss Jordan's private jet. Aven locked eyes with him and nodded, inviting him onboard.

Though they were in one hell of a hurry, he made sure to open the closest door for his teammate Sola, who was sprinting beside him despite her gorgeous crimson satin dress and matching heels. The shimmery fabric flowed out behind her, whipped by the wind from the rotors, making her look more like a goddess than a do-gooder assassin. She swatted away the hand he offered and vaulted into their ride, nearly crushing his arm in the door as she slammed it shut behind her.

Okay. So she was still pissed. And they were going to spend the next several hours locked in a tin can together before having to put their lives in each other's hands. *Perfect.*

Aarav ducked then darted around in a crouch behind the helicopter. He joined Sola in the backseat. In his lap, he clutched a military green canvas duffle and a mismatching rainbow-striped reusable shopping tote. Jordan's wife, Wren, had thrust that at him as they booked it out of their headquarters, which was currently hosting a wedding reception for two of their operatives and the woman they had pledged their lives to.

As much as Aarav wanted to smooth things over with Sola, their job had to come first. Because if he fucked that up, one or both of them might not make it back to have anything to argue about. And no way in hell was he ever going to let her get hurt because of him, or the very unwelcome disturbance his feelings for her had become lately.

If that meant she and the rest of the team thought of him as some kind of slaughter robot, devoid of emotion, then so be it. He snatched a headset from the seatback pocket and put it on even as Sola mirrored him.

"My rifle?" Aarav asked Aven, who was already taking off again.

"The flight crew was loading your sniper shit into the plane and double checking your inventory list when I left." She grunted. "It's heavy as fuck and—"

"Sensitive." Aarav figured it made him an asshole for reminding them every single time, but he couldn't afford for his scope or anything else to be even a hair out of alignment when he was taking shots from damn near a mile away.

"Must be a male gun if it needs to be babied. They can punt my kit into the cargo hold from the hanger and it'll be fine." Sola crossed her arms, which emphasized the swells of her breasts visible above the low bodice of her dress. "Or maybe Aarav gets jealous anytime someone else touches his stuff, huh?"

He groaned. How the hell was he going to get himself out of the mess he'd made with Sola? "Look, I didn't mean to chase your date away. It's not my fault he was too intimidated to stick around past the introductions to the team."

Aven whistled. "So it's going to be *that* kind of trip. I'll be sure to keep the cockpit door closed so you two can hash out your drama."

Sola whipped her loose hair over her shoulder. It might as well have lashed Aarav. Seeing her like that—gorgeous and unfettered—unlike she appeared in her typical commando gear or exercise clothes, her hair tightly braided, made him realize that just maybe he'd been ignorant to assume his feigned disinterest hadn't affected her. This woman who existed beneath the armor she usually wore around the rest of the world was vulnerable. Protective instincts combined with the lingering spikes of possessiveness and envy that had stabbed him when he'd realized she'd invited someone else, an outsider, to the wedding. Holy hell, he'd really fucked things up.

He angled to face her. "Sola, I'm sorry. Truly."

"For what?" She locked gazes with him.

Was this a test? If so, he knew the myriad ways in which he'd screwed up. The problem was, he still didn't know how to fix the issues they had. "For being who I am and for how difficult that makes it to wear my heart on my sleeve. I wish I could be more like James." He pinched the bridge of his nose as he thought of their office manager, who ran their operation as smoothly as he navigated the complex polyamorous relationship he had with his husband, wife, and former construction crew, along with the rest of their spouses. Aarav couldn't get things right with the one person he cared about, never mind nine of them. James was a genius when it came to emotions and communication.

Aven flew their helicopter as competently as she did their jet. The added agility of the aircraft made it seem as if she was chasing a hummingbird as she wove an aggressive path around Middletown before arrowing toward the private airport where their plane awaited.

He blamed her expert maneuvering for the flip-flops his stomach performed. It would have been better if that were the truth. Instead, he was pretty sure the slight relaxing of the tension around Sola's eyes at his admission was responsible for his unwelcome tingles.

"Does that mean you're willing to try to open up? Just a little?" Sola leaned toward him, her lips parting as she waited for his response. "How can I be your partner if I have no idea what you're thinking half the time?"

Aarav gulped. His fingers dug into the webbing of his duffle strap. Letting her in meant risking a lot. It wasn't like they were crossing guards. Their job came with real risks. And a much lower than average life expectancy. He'd lost most everyone he'd loved.

But the truth was, he already cared for Sola—not to mention the rest of their colleagues and friends—even if he'd refused to admit it because the idea of having them ripped away too terrified him. No matter what he did now, he was fucked.

The only thing worse than setting himself up for the inevitable, excruciating pain of grief would be disappointing Sola in the meantime. Damn it. So he scrunched his eyes closed, then nodded. "Yeah. I'll try."

And when he opened them again, it was to her beautiful lips tipped up on one side in the hint of a smile that was more pronounced given the glossy lipstick she'd worn for their friends' special occasion. He swore to himself then that he'd do his best to return her expression to the full-on beam she'd had not too long ago when she'd been inspiring his wicked thoughts as she danced with Kennedy, Ruby, and some of the other women who were part of the Shields team and their greater sphere of friends including the Powertools, Hot Rods, and Hot Rides.

Sola covered his hand with hers and pried his fingers out of the death grip he had on his duffle. She relaxed him and entwined her hand with his, promising him silently that whatever shit they got themselves into, she would remain by his side through it. He believed her. That faith was probably what had allowed his damned feelings to bubble up around her in the first place.

"Sorry to interrupt." Aven cleared her throat as they began their descent onto the tarmac. She tapped her ear, making them aware they had company on the comms. "Jordan needs you to conference in with him for a briefing. The secure video link is already open and waiting for you in the cabin of the jet. My flight crew and I will take care of everything else."

"Thanks." Sola nodded to Aven, then unbuckled the instant the chopper kissed the ground. The landing was so graceful and smooth, Aarav hardly noticed given the pounding of his heart. Sola hopped down and adjusted her dress before climbing the stairs to the waiting jet as if she were a starlet arriving on a red carpet instead of a hit woman about to board a flight to an execution.

"Hey." Aven got his attention, stopping Aarav from

following on Sola's heels.

"Yeah?"

"I've never seen her like this. Unsure. Whatever you have to do, get her head in the game before you come back down those stairs." Aven jerked her head toward where Sola had vanished, making her long, strawberry-blond hair swing on either side of her pale face dotted with freckles. "Neither of you can afford that. You have to trust each other completely or this isn't going to work. I don't like transporting dead bodies. The blood stains are hell to get out of that cream upholstery."

"I know. Fuck. I know." Aarav scrunched his eyes closed. That had been the problem all along and it was only worse now. So maybe his tactic of trying to ignore the attraction zinging between them hadn't been the right call. Maybe he needed to consider a new strategy.

Like burning his lust out of his system before they got to their destination. Damn Jordan for putting the idea of joining the mile high club in his mind earlier. What kind of boss did that?

One who cared for his agents as more than employees. That's who.

Aven shut off the helicopter and removed her headset. "It's a long flight. You'll have plenty of time to get your shit together before the mission."

Aarav realized he didn't even know where they were headed. In a way, it didn't matter. But he needed to find out exactly how to best transform into the weapon Jordan and the Shields needed him to be that day.

So he juggled his duffle and the tote, which looked to be brimming with portions from the banquet they were missing out on, then hightailed it after Sola.

When he ducked through the opening into the

luxurious aircraft, their boss was already on the monitor situated across from the couch in the lounge area along one wall of the plane. Aarav tossed his bags onto a captain's chair, then took a seat next to Sola on the supple leather Aven had been so protective of, letting his hand caress it to distract himself from the heat of Sola's satin-covered thigh pressed to his.

Behind Jordan, who looked every bit the movie star version of a spy in his tux and the elegant watch his husband and wife had given him at their own wedding, a flash of unnatural red hair made it clear their geek girl tech extraordinaire, Ruby, was also missing some of the party to help out. She beamed their images to Sola and Aarav via a secure transmission from Jordan's office.

"Can we get going? I didn't like the way Ace was eying my cake." Ruby flashed them a wink, though it was obvious she was only teasing. None of them would shirk their responsibility for taking out the world's trash to protect the innocent.

"Girl, it isn't your dessert he's hungry for." Sola snorted.

"You don't want to start that with me." Ruby straightened her replica elven tiara as she glanced between Sola and Aarav. Never piss off a nerd.

"Fair enough." Sola cracked her knuckles. "Where we going, boss?"

"Greece." Jordan got right down to business. "In exactly twelve hours, Cash Kalykalaos will be cutting the ribbon for a new casino called Dionysus's Playground on a small island, which his father just happens to own, in the Aegean Sea."

"You're sending us on vacation?" Aarav highly doubted this was going to be fun and games for anyone.

"I don't gamble." Sola crossed her arms.

"No, we're not taking chances today or any other," Jordan assured them. "I apologize for the short notice, but Cash almost never attends public events and only announced his presence at this ceremony to the high rollers less than two hours ago. When the agency that hired us spotted the ribbon on an open air balcony, they knew we'd have a shot at finally nailing this bastard."

"I don't get it." Sola tipped her head. "Are they forcing people to waste their life savings? Rigging the games even more than usual?"

"No." Jordan frowned. "There are plenty of valid whales playing there, and at the family's other casinos across Europe and the Middle East, voluntarily."

"So what's this guy done that justifies eliminating him?" Aarav already mentally calculated his odds of success for a shot at a man on a balcony of a casino on a tiny island surrounded by something other than solid ground. This was going to be a bitch.

"Their gambling operations are a front for a money laundering operation. They clean cash from a massive network of arms dealers linked to terrorism in more than thirty countries. Their latest customer was responsible for the bombing that killed one hundred and thirty-nine innocents including seventeen children in a market in Marrakesh last month. If we can cut off their access to their profits, we can make them a hell of a lot less motivated to trade this stuff in the first place."

"I'm with you now." Sola grimaced.

"Okay, so. The event is in twelve hours." Aarav checked his own watch. It wasn't flashy like Jordan's and was scratched all to hell, but it was every bit as prized a possession. "How long does it take to get there?"

"Ten to the airport on the mainland and another forty-five minutes by boat." Jordan pinched the bridge of his nose. "It's not ideal, but we'll have to make it work. This is the only chance there's been in over two years of reconnaissance to get this bastard. Aarav, we've secured a position for you on a neighboring island. Well, that's a generous description. It's more like a big chunk of rock with some wind-blown trees. But it faces the balcony and is in range. Barely."

"And me?" Sola wondered.

"We scored an invitation for you to attend the grand opening in place of a billionaire's daughter you bear a striking resemblance to in case the conditions turn out to be impossible for Aarav." Jordan frowned.

So did Aarav. Because as much as he wanted to promise both Sola and his boss that he would get that fucker no matter what, shooting at that range across open water and who knew what kind of wind conditions that came with sniping over the sea instead of land was sure to be a challenge. Even for him.

"I don't like her going in alone." Aarav would have said that about any of his teammates, but he could no longer deny that his bond with Sola amplified his concern.

"It's risky enough to plant a single operative." Jordan sighed. "And it *is* dangerous, I'm not going to lie."

"Guys, we do hazardous shit every day. It's fine. I'm probably going to be sipping champagne while that asshole's skull explodes and then I'll bail in the confusion afterward. No problem. And if there *is* one, I'll take care of it."

Jordan nodded tightly. "I know you will."

Then he jerked a thumb over his shoulder toward the wall of his office, which adjoined with James's. "James is sending the details of the locations, timing, and the transports along with maps, pictures of the targets, weather reports, and whatever other intel we can gather. But you've got plenty of time to spare while in transit. So I recommend you take a couple hours to rest and...*recover*... before you study the dossier."

Aarav heard what his boss hadn't said loud and clear. It was going to take every ounce of their abilities to pull this off and ensure neither of them was caught. Every last wrinkle he'd caused between them had to be ironed out before they attempted this assassination.

From the background, Ruby was studying them. She flicked her gaze from Sola to Aarav, then bit her lip. "See you both back home tomorrow."

Could everyone read them that easily? Having friends who were super spies made it difficult to hide personal drama.

"Yes, we will." Jordan stared at each of them for a few seconds before nodding, then ending the call. The screen turned black.

"Well, shit." Sola stood and wandered toward the cabin at the rear. Her stilettos sank into the light carpet, making it appear as though she were stabbing a cloud as she walked. Uncertain, as he had been for months, about how to bring up the tension fizzling between them, Aarav pursued her where he'd often gone the opposite direction in the past.

When she stepped inside the doorway, they both froze as if they hadn't shared this same space any number of times before when exhausted after an assignment.

"We could take turns." Aarav kicked himself for the croak his suggestion made as it tumbled from his throat.

"You know sleeping, especially in shifts, isn't what

Jordan had in mind, right?" Sola rolled her eyes at Aarav over her bare shoulder. "And I'm not worried about lying next to you on a ginormous mattress. I'm more concerned that I could hop on there naked and you'd still pretend like you don't notice the desire that's only getting stronger between us no matter how much you continually piss me off."

"Uh, yeah. Yeah, I get that." He stepped closer even though he should have marched out and taken the seat farthest away from her before concentrating on studying the intricacies of the mission no matter what anyone else recommended.

"Yet you still plan to do exactly nothing about it, right?" Sola kicked off her shoes more forcefully than required. She dropped a few inches in height yet still had one or maybe two on him.

He didn't answer her question, because he was afraid he might cave to instinct and confirm her suspicions. Instead he closed the gap between them and slipped her hair over her shoulders to her front. His fingers trembled as he reached for the zipper of her dress between her shoulder blades. She'd been heading for the elevators to their neighboring apartments when they'd gotten word the chopper was in sight of the building and diverted to the roof for pickup instead.

"I'm glad you didn't have time to change."

"Yeah, this outfit will work nicely for the grand opening of some fancy private casino." She sighed. "Maybe someone there will appreciate me."

"Fuck the assignment." Aarav figured if she was already going to be irritated with him, he might as well say what he was thinking. He knew he was playing with fire when he leaned in and murmured in her ear, "I meant because you're gorgeous. In this dress, and out of it."

To his surprise, she didn't whack him with her clutch or stab him with one of her discarded stilettos. She paused, her breath hitching, as he slid the zipper down to the small of her back. Only when it was fully open—the gorgeous curves and dips of her body fully exposed—did she turn, incredibly slowly, toward him. Her hands crossed over her chest to keep the satin from baring her breasts since he'd seen for himself she wasn't wearing a bra.

"You think so?" Her mascaraed lashes cast dark shadows on her pale cheeks as she glanced down when she asked.

He'd never seen her timid before, not even when facing some of the most evil elements of humanity hand-to-hand. This is what he'd done to her and he hated it.

"I always have." He stepped even closer, until there wasn't any space left between them and she had to have been able to feel the proof of his arousal beneath his suit. His hands cupped her shoulders.

"It sure hasn't seemed like it." She looked up then and swallowed. "I'm not used to being desperate and I don't fucking care for it either."

"I know. I'm sorry." He could apologize a million times and the words alone wouldn't mean anything to her. He had to stand by them and act accordingly. He'd never been so scared in his entire life. Not even when one of their targets had slipped around behind them and missed blowing Aarav's head off by less than six inches.

If Sola hadn't been there that day, he wouldn't be standing in front of her now.

He owed it to her to be brave and to make this leap

that the rest of their friends kept encouraging him to take.

"Do you trust Jordan? And the whole team?" Aarav blew out a sigh. "And me even though I haven't given you much reason to lately?"

"Yes." She answered before he'd even finished asking.

"Then let's do it. What they're all thinking we should. Let's get this out of our systems and keep it from fucking up our jobs." Aarav didn't think that's how it would work or he'd have done it months ago. He wasn't like the rest of the Shields or their Powertools friends in Middletown. Sex wasn't something he took lightly or indulged in casually. In fact...

"I thought you'd never ask." Sola grinned slowly, licking her lips as she leaned into him, letting go of her dress to wrap her arms around his neck instead. They were so warm and soft, he nearly melted. "I mean literally I thought you'd never ask."

Aarav grimaced. There were so many reasons he'd held back. Their careers. The complexity it was going to add to their lives. Oh yeah, and a severe lack of experience. Vanity had played a part.

"There's something you should know first." He cleared his throat. Maybe she would change her mind when he admitted the truth. Maybe she wouldn't want him after all.

"What?" She smirked. "We're both healthy. At least I've had clear reports from Kennedy every time and I assume you have too."

"Oh. Uh. Yeah." He cleared his throat and stared at the curved ceiling before admitting, "I'd have had to had sex before to have an STI."

"What are you trying to say?" Sola blinked, her head canting to the side. "You're a virgin?"

2

———

"Yeah." Aarav shuffled from one foot to the other feeling like a fool. Why would a woman like her be interested in him when he didn't even know how to please her? As lame as *Jake* had been, her bullshit date probably had at least been capable of having a one-night stand.

"Why?" Sola tipped her head, not in judgment but in an attempt to understand. "I know for a fact women drool over you all the time. I'm going to punch one of them in the boob sooner or later."

He chuckled at that, cupping her cheek. It felt natural and normal and forbidden all at once. It lent him the courage to give her the truthful answer she deserved.

"For a long time I thought I wasn't built like other people, certainly not other guys. I would never get turned on by random people or sexy scenes on TV or whatever. It wasn't until you..." He waved at his obvious erection straining against the front of his pants. "I was talking to James about it one day—"

Their office manager and team confidant knew a shit

ton about sexuality given that he was part of a pansexual polyamorous group. The Powertools believed in love in every variety.

"Why didn't you talk to me about it?" Sola asked, the hurt returning to her eyes. "I would have listened. I *wanted* to know."

"It took me a minute to figure it all out. Anyway, James said there are some people who are demisexual. They're only sexually attracted to people they have an emotional connection with. So, uh, you're the first person...you know."

Aarav did his best to sound casual. Like that revelation hadn't been a profound turning point in his life. He'd darted up to his apartment and done endless research after James had dropped that bomb, and everything he'd read had confirmed that might just be what people called someone like him. Not a freak, as he'd labeled himself for far too long.

It had shocked him at first, when he'd realized that when he hung out with Sola, for the first time in his life, he wondered what it would be like to take her to bed.

"So that means...?" Sola's gaze met his squarely then and her frown was replaced with a brilliant smile. "You don't only want me, but you *like* me too?"

"I'm sorry you don't already know that." Aarav realized fully how selfish he'd been to allow his fear of admitting it to either of them to injure her pride and her confidence.

"And you'd be willing to let me be your first?" She leaned toward him.

Only. Even he was smart enough not to say that out loud yet for fear of replacing the smoldering stare she was aiming in his direction with one of awkward disentanglement. But he couldn't imagine there ever being another woman so perfectly made for him as she was. So instead he simply nodded.

"Wow. That's...an honor. Thank you." Sola melted into him, hugging him tight. As he embraced her in return he couldn't believe he'd withheld this sense of absolute...*rightness*...from them both for months.

"So you're not mad it took me so long to finally tell you?"

"I was never angry." She raised her head from his shoulder and nipped at his lower lip. "I was frustrated."

He found he liked the edge of discomfort along with whatever else she was doing to his body by being this primal and honest, putting her needs on full display for him. Sola didn't expose her weaknesses any more easily than he did. It was the ultimate demonstration of faith.

And he wasn't going to let her down.

Not again.

"Not tonight, you won't be. Tell me what you like and I'll do it. I'll make it as good for you as I can." Aarav reached for her, but she shifted out of his hold.

She stepped back a few inches and let her dress slip to the floor where it framed her like a blood-red rose. She kicked it aside, making him gawk at her lacy red panties, the only thing left between him and all of her. Her body was flawless, strong with hints of boyishness—her eight-pack giving his a run for its money—but perfect in his eyes.

Sola was capable, tough, and ruthless when she needed to be. She was a survivor—a prerequisite for any partner of his. Because it was terrifying enough to give his heart to a badass like her, never mind someone who couldn't take care of themselves and might leave him like his family had.

"No. We're not going to do that tonight." Sola kissed him then, drawing his full attention back to her and the moment. Blowing his mind with the simple press of her lips to his, another first. One he hoped desperately would not be a last. "You've done too much thinking these past months and not enough feeling."

He nodded. "I'm sorry."

"Stop apologizing and make up for it. Now." Sola bunched his crisp dress shirt in her fists and ripped the sides apart, sending buttons pinging off the mirror attached to the back of the door.

He stared down as she unknotted his tie, leaving the ends of the maroon silk dangling over the expanse of his chest in the opening between the white panels of fabric. He couldn't stifle a groan as she kissed her way down his sternum and over his abs, her fingers curling in his waistband.

It didn't turn him on to see her on her knees in front of him, but he couldn't deny what she was doing to his libido when she cupped his cock through his pants before unzipping them. She shoved them down his hips and swiped his underwear away, leaving him bare before her in a matter of moments.

"Mmm." She stroked his cock, making him growl as her fist surrounded him with heat and softness and sure movements of her fingers over his length.

"What have you imagined this moment would be like?" she asked quietly as her fingers roamed to his balls, caressing and weighing them before tapping his cock against her parted lips.

"Nothing as powerful as this." He gasped when she licked a line up the underside of his shaft, making his eyes roll back in his head. "Maybe if I'd realized..."

She smiled, then swallowed him slowly but deliberately until she held the majority of his length in her mouth. If he'd thought her hand was warm, this...this was hell. Because as much as he wanted her to continue, he knew just like the first day back at the gym after an injury had sidelined him, he was going to need to work on his stamina if he had any chance of doing this right.

She pulled off him, making him curse. His hands automatically fisted in her hair, instinctively keeping her close. Sola looked up at him. "I want to make tonight memorable for you."

"I'll never forget a single instant of being with you like this," he promised, because it was true. He'd dreamed of it, yet never believed it would be real.

"In that case..." She swallowed him again, this time not stopping with a single pass. She began to move over him, her mouth and tongue tugging, licking, sucking, and massaging him with wet heat.

Aarav had an out of body experience, watching himself enjoy her ministrations while fireworks illuminated every nerve ending in his cock. No, his whole body. Heart included.

It might have been seconds, or minutes, but soon he realized each muscle he had was tensed and gathering to explode.

"Fuck." He swore his thighs were trembling when she put her hands on them, squeezing and bracing him so he didn't collapse and squash her beneath his weight.

There was only so much he could take and he refused to disappoint her again.

"Stop. Sola." He tugged on her hair, making her purr before she realized his intention. Damn.

"Change your mind?" she asked as she wiped her

mouth on the back of her hand, nibbling the corner of her lips instead of him.

"Not at all. I've waited too long for this moment for it to be over in five seconds."

She beamed up at him, then rose, taking his hand and tugging him toward the bed. "Well, if you need a timeout, I know the perfect distraction."

She climbed onto the bed and rested her shoulders against the hill of pillows at the top, spreading her legs and teasing her pussy with one of her middle fingers. No way was he about to resist an invitation like that.

Aarav dove between her legs with enthusiasm if not finesse. He dragged his teeth up her cut thighs before his mouth landed on her pussy. Her fingers speared into his thick onyx hair and used it as a grip, directing his lips and tongue to where they'd do her the most good.

He'd barely gotten a taste of her sweet pussy when Aven came across the plane's intercom. "Prepare yourselves. We're about to take off."

"Yes. Yes, we are." Sola didn't even try to disguise the obvious desire dripping from her breathy response.

Should they have been in one of the proper seats with their belts fastened? Yes. Was either of them about to stop just to follow the rules? Hell no. They were shattering every boundary they'd set between them since joining the Shields. If they died, at least it would be a spectacular way to go out.

The acceleration of the plane down the runway shoved Aarav tighter against Sola's flesh, his nose nudging her clit as his tongue probed inside her. He reached up with one hand, squeezing her breast while he latched onto her pussy and began to suck.

His other hand sought her entrance and worked two

fingers inside her, marveling at the damp silk that drew on his digits like her mouth had his cock so recently. When he groaned, she clamped down on him.

And as the plane left the ground, launching itself into flight, Sola joined it.

She shouted his name and her nails scored a path along his shoulders, only making his dick harder where it bored into the mattress as they climbed above the clouds.

When her spasms slowed, he tried to soothe her swollen flesh with long laps of his tongue. It only seemed to make her tense and shudder more.

Sola was still panting, her eyes glassy when she shoved his shoulder, urging him to his back.

He thought she might want to be held as she recovered from what had seemed to be a powerful orgasm, so it surprised him—though it probably shouldn't have—when she straddled him instead, her drenched pussy sliding along the length of his shaft.

This was it. The moment he had both dreaded and then convinced himself didn't matter when he imagined it would never arrive.

Then and there he was willing to admit that had been a big fat lie he'd told himself in the dark.

"Don't feel pressured." She petted his chest, then leaned forward to kiss him sweetly. "Are you sure?"

"Yeah," was all he could say before she sat up and guided his cock to her entrance. Sola stared straight into his eyes as she joined them, sheathing him as she sank onto his thighs.

The sensation was potent and life altering. No wonder other people did this all the time with whoever was interested. Aarav's voice was strangled when he rasped, "You're killing me."

He clutched the sheets to anchor himself when it seemed like he could keep ascending straight into orbit. What the hell was she doing to him, hugging him within her, introducing him to wonders he couldn't possibly have understood without experiencing them himself?

"It's only going to get better," Sola promised as she began to ride him, glorious as her muscles were put to better use than running pointless miles for conditioning or holding still for hours when ambushing a target.

This was what she'd been made for. She was fluid grace and passionate beauty as she rose and fell over him, her hips arcing as she rubbed herself against his torso, taking pleasure even as she doled it out.

"Yeah, like that." She coached him with moans that let him know every time he did something right. Each one of them reverberated through him, amplifying the bliss of her flesh fisted around his cock. When she began to tighten around him and fuck faster, he held his breath, forcing himself to resist the lure of her body and her mounting pleasure.

"You don't have to hold out. I'm already good. You did a damn fine job of getting me off." Sola sighed and squeezed her breast as if it were as heavy as his balls felt right then.

Aarav took his cues from her, reaching up to replace her fingers, pinching her nipples until she shuddered around him and he began to glide in and out of her even easier.

"No. You go." Aarav found it wasn't chivalry speaking but need. He had to see her enjoying it or there wasn't any point. "I can't come if you don't. At least once more. Let me see what this does to you."

"If you insist." Sola closed her eyes and sucked her

lower lip between her teeth, concentrating on the reawakened pleasure blossoming within her.

Aarav reached around her and palmed her ass with one hand, using the grip to help her grind on him each time she bottomed out, fusing them as tightly as possible. He couldn't believe this was happening and that he seemed to be capable of bringing bliss to a woman as worldly and beautifully brazen as her.

The instant she unraveled around him, mewling his name as she shuddered and wrung his cock, something triggered within Aarav. A facet of himself he'd never suspected was lurking beneath his doubts and seeming non-emotion exploded to the surface. He put his hands around her waist and tossed them to their sides. Good thing the plane was banking in the correct direction or they would have tumbled to the floor. Either way, he wouldn't have stopped. She was still coming as he flipped her the rest of the way over and began to fuck.

Aarav might never have done it before, but his body knew how. It followed the rhythm she'd taught him when she'd ridden him, pounding into her over and over.

It didn't take long, but when she opened her eyes and beamed up at him, obviously smug and satisfied for breaking through his restraint, he lost it. Aarav roared and sank into her as deeply as he could. His balls drew up tight to his body and come launched from them, saturating her pussy with his release.

It had been a sprint, not a marathon, but there was no denying both of them had reached the finish line together. He twitched as aftershocks of rapture zinged from his toes to the tips of his fingers and especially to the important parts in between—like his dick and his heart.

"Oh, fuck." He groaned. What had they done?

It might be casual for her, a way to vent some steam, but that wasn't how he worked and he wasn't sure she'd fully understood when she'd volunteered to take his V-card.

When worry helped erase the last of his erection, he slipped from Sola and crashed to the mattress next to her. She hummed and curled up beside him, one leg flung over his and her forearm planted on his chest as she studied him intently.

"Are you *sure* you've never done that before?" Her smile was full and languid as she ruffled his hair then feathered it out of his eyes.

"Positive." He grinned at her despite the circumstances. Because there was no denying that she'd made his first time memorable enough that if it turned out to be his only time, he'd be fine with that. He supposed this was where things should either turn more intimate, in the case of true lovers, or he should stop being so damn clingy, if this had been a simple hook-up.

Not that he was capable of that, but he imagined that would be the case if he was.

Sensing his awkwardness, Sola separated them. She stretched and peeked over toward the window where only the sky, complete with the amber and pink-swirled puff of clouds above the setting sun added to the surreal ambiance in the cabin. "I've never done it on a plane, so I guess you could say it was a first for me too."

"I appreciate you trying to make me feel better about that." He winced. "I hope it wasn't a total disaster for you."

"I'll give you that since you don't have anything to compare to." Sola glared, putting him on familiar ground. "But yeah, that was not the way a woman responds if it's just so-so."

He nodded. Grateful for that, at least. Because she'd shifted his entire foundation and he would never be the same again.

When the silence stretched a little too long, Sola asked, "Was there food in that bag Wren gave you before?"

"Yeah, let me get it for you." Aarav rolled from bed without bothering to put on his clothes. He strutted from the bedroom to grab the tote full of dinner and dessert.

"I like this look on you." Sola licked her lips when he returned, and it made him wonder if she was hungry for what he was carrying or for more of him. Food would have to do. Even a thirty-year dry spell couldn't leave him ready to go again so quickly.

"Thanks." He settled beside her and drew her into his lap before kissing her over and over. If nothing else, that simple pleasure was one he wasn't ready to quit indulging in so soon. Her lips were full and warm against his as she gave as good as she got. "It's because of you. No one else has ever made me feel like...this."

He stopped short of identifying his feelings, though he already had a damn good idea what it was trying to puff up his chest to three times its normal size.

"I like that, you know. Being special to you." Sola nuzzled his bearded jaw.

And suddenly something he'd agonized over, the fear that his lack of experience might drive her away once she found out, vanished. How had she managed to make it seem like a benefit instead of a drawback?

Aarav grinned, then started rummaging through the containers in the bag. He set them out on the bed in front of them. Steak. Fish. Sides. Bread. And dessert. Bingo. "You want real food?"

"Hell no. I like skipping straight to the good stuff."

Sola popped open the lid on the chocolate cake oozing black cherry filling. Their friend Morgan had baked it especially for Sevan, Ransom, and Levi. It was decadent and dark and tangy yet still sweet in the center of all those layers. Just like Sola.

Aarav picked up a morsel with his fingers and fed it to her, loving how she spent more time than necessary licking and sucking his fingers clean.

"More." She opened her mouth and waited for him to give her another bite. Then she surprised him by returning the favor. Nothing had tasted as good in his entire life. He thought, if the universe paid him back even a tiny bit for all the hurt it had put him through in his childhood, he would ask Morgan to make the same cake the day he got up the nerve to propose to Sola.

Because he could see it in a flash. That's where they could end up. If their jobs and the evil in the world didn't rip them apart first. The reminder was like a bucket of ice water dumped over his head.

"Shit. We should study the file." He groaned and reached for his duffle, withdrawing the tablet inside even as Sola smacked his ass.

"I've always wanted to do that. You have such a cute butt." She grinned, then dove at him, licking the partial icing handprint she'd left on his flank to keep it from staining the sheets.

"Uh, thanks." He shook his head and forced himself to concentrate. That wasn't usually an issue for him. He could turn off everything but the feel of his rifle, the brush of wind against the hairs on his forearm, and whoever was in his sights, then lie in wait for hours. Days, if need be.

But in that moment, he couldn't take his eyes from Sola even as she turned on the device he'd already forgotten about and started flipping through virtual documents.

Killing wasn't easy, even when it was deserved. What Sola did was damn difficult. Bearing that burden, for the sake of the innocents it would protect, was a sacrifice not many other people could understand. But he did.

Maybe that was part of why he'd refused to acknowledge his feelings for her for so long. She took risks. And so did he by letting himself care for her.

As Aarav studied her—naked, sitting cross legged, the container of cake balanced on one knee and the tablet with the information they needed to pull off their assignment on the other—he knew he'd made a horrific mistake. Because there was no way in hell one time with Sola was ever going to be enough to burn her out of his system. Instead, the flame she'd ignited in him only blazed brighter.

It was several hours later, after they had locked in their plans and there was nothing to do but wait, that she finally noticed his hungry gaze. "You want more cake?"

"There's something else I'd rather have seconds of." He pounced on her, making her squeal and laugh... though it wasn't long before her giggles were replaced with moans.

If the mission went sideways and he died later that day, at least he'd go happy.

3

———

Sola passed the guard with her attempt at a sultry smile, then flipped her hair over her shoulder. Not because she was vain, but because it gave her the perfect cover to reactivate her comms after having made it through security. Awfully comfortable in this glass fortress they'd built, they hadn't even frisked her for a weapon. Fools. "I'm in."

"Good." James spoke into her ear from most of the way around the world. "There isn't much time. Aarav is finalizing his gear set up, so we'll need you to try for a visual on the target. Stick close in case we need you to step in."

Maybe it was the flight on the private jet. Or the ride she'd taken on Aarav. Twice. Or the glamorous dress and jewels she was wearing for once. But for some reason, she felt every bit a super spy worthy of a feature film instead of the imposter she'd sometimes considered herself when surrounded by a team of incredible men and women.

She hated to admit it, but Aarav's apparent lack of interest in her over the past several months, when she swore she could feel their bond growing by the second, had completely fucked with her self-confidence. Not to mention her faith in her gut instincts.

That could be a fatal flaw for a field agent like her, especially a lone wolf assassin deep in enemy territory. Out here, all she had to rely on was herself. Sure, Aarav was aiming a monstrous gun at the balcony—or would be shortly—but if shit went down, she would be on her own to extract herself from the flaming dumpster fire this place would quickly turn into.

With that in mind, Sola verified the intel they'd gotten in the form of the casino blueprints. The exits were as indicated on them, placed at each of the four cardinal directions around the glass dome that encapsulated the gaming tables. It wasn't an act when she gawked at the sparkling panels that cast rainbows onto the black marble flooring and allowed the gorgeous seascape around them to make a perfect backdrop for distracting someone from the thousands they were losing by the second.

Sola noted her possible escape paths as she circled the room under the guise of browsing the refreshments that lined the perimeter of the space. She had worked up a bit of an appetite that not even leftovers in bed from Sevan, Ransom, and Levi's wedding had been able to fully satisfy. So she plucked a cracker topped with some brown stuff that looked horrid but tasted divine from a filigreed silver platter and was immediately met with a roving server offering her a linen napkin to wipe her fingers on afterward.

"Thank you." She cleaned her hands, then accepted a flute of champagne from yet another of the staff. They probably outnumbered the guests.

"Any sign of Cash yet?" Jordan asked, though he could

see the room as well as her given the camera embedded among the diamonds and rubies of her necklace. The thing was practically microscopic yet relayed images both in ultra high definition and alternate imaging like infrared, for identifying the heat signatures of hidden bodies. It came in handier in jungles than in casinos, but it never hurt to have as much information as possible. Jordan didn't skimp for his operatives. He gave them every tool possible to ensure a positive outcome for their missions. With the prices he charged the government agencies they worked for, they could afford it.

"Nope." Sola hid the movement of her lips behind the napkin. "But Daddy's right over there."

She angled her torso so that he was clearly in sight. When she did, she could hear the furious clicks of Ruby banging away on one of her keyboards in the command center, probably taking screen captures for their files, which some analyst would scour for useful data later.

"Who the hell names their kid Cash anyway? Sounds kind of douchey." Sola let her gaze lift long enough to take in the man who owned this empire, at least according to official documents. If his kid was as much of a dirtbag as their informants promised, then his father was merely a puppet.

"Someone who raises a child to care about wealth over everything else." James's voice seemed to shudder at that. "Even the lives of innocent children hoping for a piece of candy when their parents are finished shopping. Someone who created a monster."

Right. Sola reminded herself why she was there. As fascinating as it was in this crystalline globe dotted with billionaires and sharks, her job wasn't to people watch. Except something about Cash's dear old dad kept drawing her gaze. He was surrounded by gorgeous women, all of them together probably not much more than him in age. And the way he sat—reclined, splayed, and completely inattentive—spoke of power and sloth. If he was a puppet, he was a damn good one.

She would have asked Jordan a few more specific questions about the man if she'd had some cover, but just then an admittedly handsome man in a tuxedo approached. "Not too shabby, huh?"

It had been so long since she'd flirted with someone, Sola had to dig deep. She hit him with a dazzling smile and a bit of innuendo as she let her gaze wander over his fine form. "Not at all."

"I'll be playing at the high-limit blackjack tables if you want to come cheer me on. I could use a good luck charm like you when I start bidding at a hundred thousand a pop." Oh, blech. Did women really fall for that?

Sola tuned out as he tried to strike up a conversation with her. Mostly about how much money he'd brought to flush down the toilet at the inaugural run of the tables.

If she'd ever found men like him attractive, she couldn't possibly anymore after she'd gotten to know Aarav. He might not be as tall as the guy in front of her or as debonair, but he was an unpretentious compact ball of muscle and raw, naked energy.

Compared to Aarav, this guy appealed as much as flat, grocery store champagne would have after whatever the hell expensive shit she was sipping.

As if her thoughts drew him, Aarav came across the comms, making her heart speed up in a way this man hitting on her had no chance of doing no matter what small country it was he seemed to practically own. "I'm in place. This is sketchy as fuck, but I think I can make it work. The wind is gusty. We'll have to hope it settles down, even for a few seconds, when we need it to most."

"You've got this." Jordan never doubted his Shields, even when they weren't so sure of themselves. And he'd never been wrong yet. Not about their capabilities and not about the subjects of their hunts. So Sola dusted off her unease with one last glance at Cash's father, who was staring in return.

Shit. The very last thing she wanted to do was draw attention to herself.

Sola smiled at the man across from her and lifted her glass. "Excuse me. Need to go fix my lipstick after this."

Before he replied, she had already left him behind, heading toward the balcony for a better view of their main stage. The entire casino seemed like a reverse snow globe, surrounded by three hundred sixty degree views of the cerulean sea beyond a brief tumble of greenery and boulders down to the waves surrounding them. It could have been gorgeous if it weren't built from the blood of innocents.

"Yo, Jordan. Are we *sure* the dad's not dirty too? He's giving me bad vibes and gross looks from across the room. Maybe I can take him out before I bail in the confusion of things afterward..."

"That's not the plan. It's too dangerous to add objectives now." The response came not from Jordan, but from Aarav. "But if he looks at you like that again, I won't feel bad about sending two bullets that way instead of one."

"That's not necessary." Jordan weighed in. "We have no reason to believe he's involved. Every bit of intel we have says it's Cash who's made the deal with these devils."

With two against one, Sola squashed the tendrils of

doubt trying to grow within her as she had with similar feelings about her relationship with Aarav these past months. Her team was right. Nothing fucked up an operation worse than an agent going rogue and deviating from the plan. Sola clicked her comms twice to indicate her agreement.

Jordan continued as if reading and she could hear papers fluttering in the background. Was he double-checking the information they'd been given? She wouldn't doubt it. He was meticulous with both their objectives and with the safety of his operatives. Probably because he'd lost a lover to an ambush on assignment back when he worked for the government, which now hired them to do their dirty work in the gray areas of the law.

Jordan continued, "This all started because Cash likes to take odds he shouldn't. He's a wild card. Too risky. And when he made book on a giant international match and the underdog won in some fluke, he ended up having to strike a deal with the gunrunners to keep afloat without letting his father figure out how much trouble they were really in. Once you get tangled up in that shit, it's awfully hard to get out again. If he even wanted to."

"Damn it." Sola rubbed her hand over the hairs trying to stand up on the back of her neck. She had to keep her focus and resist distraction simply because Cash's father was slimy, if not evil.

As she faced out the window, imagining Aarav splayed, clinging to the top of some cliff as he lined up the casino in his sights, a movement in the corner near the door out to the landing caught her attention.

"Got him." She stood straighter as she squinted, trying to get a better look at a man who was already dead, even if he didn't know it yet. He was somewhere between Aarav and the guy who'd been hitting on her in height, lean but well-muscled, with short dark hair and a beard that would have reminded her of Aarav's if it had been somewhat wild instead of neat and tidy.

Unlike his father, Cash was alone. Tucked into what few shadows there were in the place as if he didn't care for the spotlight or the cloying attention of socialites. He scowled as he surveyed the crowd, his face only relaxing when he turned toward the waves slapping the rocky shoreline.

Sola could relate. Too bad she couldn't spend some time out there hiking with Aarav and figuring out where the hell things between them were going.

Cash huffed powerfully enough to haze the glass in front of him before letting his head fall forward and his forehead bump into the window. It wasn't the move of a man who dealt in lost souls or formed alliances with gunrunners for profit. That kind of man would never dare to show weakness while hiding from the crowds of adoring sycophants in the other room.

"Jordan?" Sola hissed, trying not to move her mouth much despite her position next to a gold pot housing a mammoth plant with fronds that dangled around her, providing some cover from onlookers.

"Yeah?" His question was clipped, as if he could sense the tension in that one word.

"You're sure? Absolutely?" She'd never questioned him before. Just...staring at the man they'd been sent to take out didn't instill her with the same sense of righteousness she usually felt on assignment. This had more in common with kicking a stray puppy.

"It went through the channels. Came from a trusted source, but with the reception and the time constraints we didn't have a chance to do as much cross-checking as usual." Jordan groaned. "Everything I've seen looks in order. Let me check on—"

James cut in. "I've got him on surveillance. Entering the balcony. Aarav, status."

"The shot is lined up," Aarav confirmed. They were about to do this. If his rifle was equipped with a laser capable of projecting that far, Cash's forehead would currently be sporting a bright red dot where there soon would be a gaping hole.

Time slowed. Sola's eyes widened when Cash glanced up and met her gaze directly.

In that instant, something passed between them. Did he know his time was limited? Did he regret the things he'd done?

"It's a shame to unalive someone so fine," Sola murmured without realizing she'd said it aloud.

"Are you trying to make me jealous?" Aarav growled, and she imagined his finger tightening on the trigger.

"No, it's just..." She couldn't identify why, but her reaction to this man was very different than those she'd had when in close proximity to previous targets. Every single one of her senses hummed, and not due to danger.

"Enough chatter," Jordan shushed them. "Aarav, you're up. Sola, are you ready?"

"I..." She looked from Cash to his father and back, her heart suddenly pounding and not because she was afraid of escaping unscathed.

Was Cash truly a beautiful demon who had been trapped in a web of his own making?

Or was he being set up to look that way by someone else?

"Wind is gone." Aarav grunted. "Now's our chance."

Every instinct she had rebelled.

Sola crossed to the balcony door and shattered their carefully laid plans by ripping it open and stepping outside. Cash didn't even bother to look at her. In a monotone voice, he rumbled, "So who'd my father piss off now?"

He got it. He'd somehow made her and he knew they were about to end him. Yet he wasn't throwing her off the balcony or sounding the alarm. When he turned toward her, resting his hip on the glass wall, waiting patiently for her to respond, she swore she could see straight into his soul.

It was time for her to stop silencing her sixth sense and listen to what her gut was telling her no matter if it cost her the job she adored or even her life. This man wasn't the one they were after. And if she let Aarav put a bullet between his gorgeous eyes, then they'd all be murderers.

"Something's not right. Stop." With that realization, she dashed across the balcony and stepped between the man who'd turned her every bone to jelly hours ago and the man they'd been sent to kill.

"HOLD! AARAV ABORT! DO NOT SHOOT!" James shouted into the comms loud enough to obliterate Sola's hearing for a few moments.

"What the fuck is she doing?" Aarav snarled distinctly before her comms erupted in a chaos of incredulous chatter.

The truth was, she had no idea what came next or how she was going to escape alive from the mess she'd just made of their mission.

4

———

Cash couldn't believe he'd let his father pressure him into playing a part in their ridiculous show. He didn't give a single fuck about this casino or any of the other establishments in his father's portfolio. The only reason he'd agreed to leave the yacht he lived on and come ashore was because he'd always had a soft spot for this island. His mother had brought him camping here once as a child. Cash had thought of asking his father for it so he could make it his home, when he'd believed settling down and having a normal life could be possible.

These days he was disillusioned by the greed and apathy of most humans, preferring to keep to himself, surrounded by nature. He'd spent three years backpacking in the Alps before commandeering one of his father's yachts and living on the ocean.

He was considering bailing no matter how much his father had pressured him to stay long enough to cut this damn ribbon on another money factory. Why the hell was it so important that he be involved?

It wasn't like his father gave a fuck about him. Never

had. And in fact, seemed to resent the reminder of Cash's mother, who died before she could be fully tamed by the bastard.

Was he an embarrassment to her memory for hiding away on his ship and turning a blind eye to how much more corrupt his father seemed every time he was forced into seeing the man again? For living simply enough off the wealth he'd inherited from her without trying to turn his father's excesses into something meaningful?

Probably.

So when he turned and caught sight of the siren in red, he didn't even flinch. The woman strode toward him and stared, her intensity nothing like the coy flirtations of the women hoping to attract his attention inside. This woman approached with intent. And aggression.

She wasn't there to charm him or be his false friend.

She was an enemy. He knew it immediately.

And didn't even care.

"So who'd my father piss off now?" He shrugged and wondered if this was it. The time he'd be offed instead of only threatened with kidnap or torture in an attempt to blackmail his father. Little did she know, that bastard wouldn't give a damn or try very hard—if at all—to reclaim his only acknowledged son. He certainly wouldn't part with a single one of his precious Euros in exchange.

The woman didn't bother to respond. Instead, she shoved her hand into an artfully concealed panel in her dress and withdrew a funky-looking white gun, probably made of plastic or ceramic to avoid detection by the metal detector.

It seemed deadly enough as he stared down its barrel.

"You can come quietly with me or I can kill you. Your

choice." She blocked the gun from sight of the guests indoors with her body.

Cash figured it said a lot about the state of his existence that he didn't really give a fuck if she pulled the trigger or not. But there was something about her, the urgency in her eyes—almost an unspoken plea—that called to him. For the first time in a long time, he didn't want to disappoint someone.

So he shrugged. "Lead the way."

"Don't try anything stupid. We have a sniper with his sights set on you. You will not leave here alive unless it's with me." As if to prove her point, the glass wall rimming the balcony—which he'd so recently been clutching as he wished he were anywhere but there—shattered into a billion dazzling shards, raining to the ground below in a deluge of prismatic rubble.

"Son of a bitch!" He jumped as the woman flew into action.

She clutched his wrist then tugged, dragging him inside even as security and curious guests began to swarm the area like angry ants, trying to figure out what the hell had happened.

"Was that really necessary, Aarav?" she grumbled to someone he couldn't see as they approached the stairway. "A bit dramatic, don't you think?"

A pause as she kicked open the fire exit door to keep from letting go of either her gun or his arm was followed by, "Yes. I realize you're pissed. Okay, fuck stealth. It's a good distraction. We're heading to the boat. Same extraction plan. See you at the plane."

Looked like they were going on a trip together. That was if his father didn't have something to say about it. As they barreled into the stairwell and chaos erupted around them, Cash looked over his shoulder in time to catch a glimpse of his father glaring in their direction before the steel door clanged shut behind them. Probably because Cash had ruined his father's party and stolen the attention from him.

"He can't save you." She yanked Cash hard enough he might have tumbled down the stairs, taking her with him if he hadn't gripped the railing with his free hand. As it was, he had no idea how she was outpacing him in those heels and with maroon silk flying all around her.

Damn, she was gorgeous. This was not the time to find a woman interesting for the first time in longer than he cared to think about. But this femme fatale with rich walnut hair and eyes to match, rimmed with gold, along with ovaries of steel...well, he wasn't too sad to be following her out of this hellhole.

"No shit." Cash practically rolled his eyes. He figured he would wait her out and take his shot at escaping once they reached whatever boat she'd mentioned to whomever she was talking to. On the water, he was in his element. He'd swim for it if it came to that. "Nor would he be likely to break a nail in order to keep my ass alive. You obviously don't know him very well."

Which was interesting. Why was she after him if it wasn't something to do with his father?

Or his father's money.

"Don't care to if he looks at all women the way I saw him ogling the ones upstairs, myself included. No thanks." They reached the ground floor and she tapped her ear. "Am I clear on the exit?"

The answer from whomever she was in communication with must have been affirmative because next thing he knew she slammed through that door too before hustling around the wild side of the island, where a cliff of at least two hundred feet plummeted straight down to the ocean below.

"The team only intended for one of us to be leaving here, so we're going to have to improvise." The woman disturbed a pile of brush at the base of the single weathered tree to uncover a freshly set metal anchor, a coiled line in perfect condition, and a high-quality climbing harness.

"We're rappelling?" He tipped forward a tad to peek at the waves beneath. There was no boat. No land. No nothing but waves from the windward side of the island. "You must be kidding."

"Have you done it before?" She crouched, preparing the webbing and holding it out for him to step into.

"Yeah, plenty." The solitude of rock climbing came close to the peace he found bobbing on the open ocean.

"Great. Get in." She grabbed his calf, her fingers squeezing his muscle for a moment before guiding it into the rigging. By force of habit he drew the harness upward, adjusted it around his package, and clipped in.

"Nice." She smiled up at him, making something rush through him that was probably shock and adrenaline but felt more like attraction. Was he so desperate for praise that he let his captor and would-be assassin manipulate his emotions? Probably.

In less than a minute he was settled in as she double-checked the gear. "Looks good."

"And how are you getting down?" He tipped his head as he bent the rope around his waist and gripped it in his brake hand.

"Tandem rappel. She took the skirt of her dress and lifted it to her waist, flashing him a glimpse of lacy red panties that he was pretty sure would have showed off her ass spectacularly if he'd seen her from behind. She used the long fabric including the train to loop around his waist and tied it off in a cumbersome knot. Though she'd done the best possible job with what she had, he wasn't convinced it would hold her toned weight. "I'm going to hang low to keep from fucking up your center of gravity. Ready?"

Shouts rang out as two men in black charged at them from the casino. They obviously cared more about stopping her than accidentally taking him out. Fuck that.

"This seems like a terrible idea."

"It is. So don't make me take one of my arms from around your waist to shoot you or those guys. Let's go." She sat on the edge of the cliff, her feet dangling above nothing, then tugged him gently backward until the rig bore his weight.

Cash fed out some rope and began walking down the rock as she hugged his waist tight. It was clunky with her dangling between his legs but manageable, so he kept going, doing everything in his power to ignore her face pressed awfully close to his groin. If someone had bet him ten million dollars back in the casino that this was how his day would end up, he would have taken the wager... and lost.

They were more than three-quarters of the way to the surface of the water before pebbles bounced around them from the approach of his father's goons.

The woman clinging to him grabbed his ass. "Faster. Almost there."

"Should we cut the rope?" one of the security guards asked.

"What? Why would they do that with you on it?" The

woman glanced up at Cash and he grimaced. This might be where she discovered he was worthless to his father. And therefore, to her.

"If you thought I was your insurance...sorry." He grunted as he skidded along ten feet or so on an undercut section of the escarpment. Her back grazed the sharp surface, but she didn't so much as flinch. "Shit. Hang on."

"Not planning on letting go," she mumbled against his abs.

Sweat beaded on his brow and rolled down his chest. Whether from the exertion or her nearness, he couldn't convincingly say.

He might have worried about it if the rope didn't start vibrating in his hand. "They're doing it. Fuck."

"Focus." She growled and he could feel her arms beginning to tremble around his hips.

Cash moved faster, less carefully, bouncing them against the cliff. They were probably about twenty feet away from the crests of the waves when the roar of an outboard engine caught his attention. "Is that our ride?"

"Yeah," she confirmed. And before he realized what she was doing, she dropped away, cannonballing into the sea.

"Holy shit!" He glanced down to find his feet could nearly touch the water, so he kicked off his shoes then let out all the line. As soon as he splashed down, she was there, clutching his shirt in her fist as if to keep him afloat. Not necessary.

It was less than a minute before someone was fishing them from the sea. The woman jammed him into the low point of the keel before throwing herself over him like a bright red wet blanket when a shot rang out from above.

"Are you trying to kill me or save me?" he asked with a grunt.

"Hell if I know anymore." She finally relaxed as whoever was driving the boat gunned the ridiculously overpowered engines and sped away from land.

It was the last thing she would say to him as they made their way to a neighboring island, picked up some dude and a giant gun—likely the one that had destroyed the balcony railing instead of Cash's brains.

She and the sniper, however, said an awful lot with the glares they exchanged during the entire bouncy, uncomfortable ride. It was far too late for Cash to change his mind, so all he could do was wonder what sort of bullshit he'd gotten himself into.

5

———————

Cash had given up asking them who the fuck they were and where they were taking him. To be honest, shouting over the noise of the engine and the slap of the aluminum hull on the waves they screamed over wouldn't have been very effective anyway. So he hunkered down, drenched and wind whipped, and tried not to shiver to death.

When they docked at a private island much lower and flatter than the one they'd smuggled him from, he spotted a private jet that rivaled something out of his father's fleet perched on the runway.

His shock and curiosity had just about worn off, replaced by discomfort and irritation. Who the fuck did these people think they were? They could have killed him on purpose or by accident. And the blood oozing from the woman's back where she'd caught the projections of the cliff did nothing to calm him either.

The instant they were within reach, she stood and leapt gracefully to the dock despite the ruined dress now plastered to her. The sniper they'd picked up shoved Cash's shoulder none too lightly. "Go on."

Cash did as he checked around for somewhere to bail to without much luck. Sandwiched between the man and woman, he marched toward the waiting jet, which was capable of whisking them off to pretty much anywhere in the world. Why?

He hesitated.

"Get in the plane," the man growled. Without the din around them, Cash noticed he had a fairly thick accent. Indian, maybe. He also happened to be nearly as hot as the woman.

Damn, what was wrong with him? Had it really been so long since he'd gotten laid that he was finding his captors attractive? It must be the leftover adrenaline coursing through his system. "Not until you tell me who you are and where we're going."

"Did you forget? I still have my gun." The woman tapped it against her hip, then gestured with the barrel at the stairs.

"You don't want to shoot me. You could have a thousand times already." Cash snorted at her.

"Yeah, but *I* sure as fuck want to." The man glared. "So don't test me. In fact..."

He slapped a restraint on Cash's wrist before he even saw it coming, then yanked it behind his back and cinched the other side. "Hey!"

"Was that really necessary?" the woman asked with a long-suffering look at the man.

"Yeah. Your pet is still dangerous." The man practically vibrated as he said it. He was *pissed* no matter how well he contained it. That sort of quiet rage was far more terrifying than overblown anger. It motivated Cash to do as he said.

Not like he had a choice.

He entered the plane, ducking through the rounded cutout in its body before glancing around. There was nowhere for him to sit without soaking the cream leather with his soggy suit. Hell, his socks squelched with every step on the plush white carpet.

A strawberry-blond woman with a fair complexion and freckles darted from the cockpit and chucked a box of garbage bags at the man who'd climbed up behind Cash. He caught it with one hand, then laid plastic on the seats for Cash and his partner.

As soon as the woman who'd abducted him entered, the blonde slammed the door closed and returned to the cockpit, locking herself in. The engine started a few moments later. They weren't wasting any time.

"Who are you?" Cash tried again. "What the hell do you want with me?"

"I admit, he's convincing." The man turned to the woman then back to Cash. He reached over and buckled Cash in to the sofa. He smelled good. Like dirt and salt spray. Up close Cash could see the cords of his neck and the definition in his chest. Damn, when was the last time he'd had a man like that in his bed? Probably never.

His father had never accepted that he was bisexual. The time he'd caught Cash making out with the landscaper's son when they were teenagers had been the first real rift in their relationship. And though the women Cash had also openly dated afterward had appeased him some, he wasn't a fool. He had to know Cash had continued to fuck men in the shadows.

At least until he'd left his father's house for his yacht, and never come back.

He cleared his throat and shook his head as if to rid his brain of the memories.

The pilot's voice came over the sound system. "The boss needs to speak with you. We're leaving. Now."

"Jordan's going to fucking fire your ass. And I don't blame him." The man rounded on the woman, who was slumped, arms crossed over her chest, probably to hide rock-hard nipples now that the plane's air-conditioning was hitting their saturated skin. He shivered too.

"Don't you trust me?" She grimaced as the TV screen on the front bulkhead flashed to life revealing a man in a suit that Cash instantly knew was the person in charge along with a few supporting staff in the background—a woman with unnaturally red hair and a toned yet thin man wearing a rainbow-striped T-shirt and tight jeans with neon yellow sneakers.

"He does. He's scared. That was dangerous shit. Even for us," the colorful guy intervened.

"Let's keep this brief until we know more." The boss was curt but calm. Again, much more terrifying than Cash's father when having a temper tantrum. "Cash, my name is Jordan. I own a security services firm called Shields. You've met Sola and Aarav already."

Sola? Aarav? They suited and were as unusual and alluring names as the people who owned them. "Security services? Is that code for hitmen?"

"He's as smart as he is pretty." The woman with the bright hair flashed a wry grin. "I'm Ruby and Rainbow Brite over there is our office manager, James."

The guy flashed him a finger wave.

What the fuck had he gotten himself into? "Who

wants me dead? Unless it's my father, I can't think of anyone who'd give enough of a fuck to hire you."

"Okay. I'm starting to see what you mean, Sola." Jordan squinted as if he was cataloging every detail about Cash. It made him want to squirm. "I'm going to use your flight time to figure out what the fuck is going on. Bring him home and we'll sort through this fucking mess."

"When you say that...you don't mean to the basement, do you?" Sola asked, her teeth scraping over the chapped and bleeding portion of her lower lip. When had she done that?

Whatever it was they kept in the lower level of their headquarters, Cash was certain he did not want to find out firsthand. It might also be the reason they weren't hiding their identities from him. If he turned out to be the enemy they'd obviously considered him, he wouldn't be leaving their facility alive.

"Damn it, Sola." Aarav flung his hands out. "Why are you so protective of him?"

"I have to have faith in my intuition instead of letting you and everyone else around here fuck with me. Something isn't adding up. And I won't let any of you, my family, do something you will regret." She sat up straighter then, even if the crinkle of wet plastic took away a smidgeon of her clout.

"Damn straight. What have I been telling you for months?" James was grinning while everyone else was dour. "This has been a breakthrough trip, hasn't it?"

He peered between Sola and Aarav, measuring them. Cash knew what he was thinking because he was wondering the same thing. Aarav's possessiveness was dialed up to eleven. There was no way they were simply co-workers, or even friends.

They must be lovers.

Fuck. That was hot and also bad news for Cash, lusting after them both.

"Yeah. Maybe. Who knows?" Sola looked out the window as they began to taxi for takeoff. "We can talk about it when we get home."

"Don't let your guard down," Jordan warned his operatives. "Until we know for sure, keep him under watch and bound. See you soon."

He hesitated before disconnecting the call. "For the record, Sola, I would never fire you for making that kind of call." He grew quieter then, but not softer. "If I'd listened to Johnny's premonition that something was off all those years ago, he might still be here today. You did good."

Sola blinked a few times and gave Jordan a curt nod. Then he was gone, the screen blank.

But that didn't clear the air between her and Aarav, which was still dense enough to risk bringing the plane down even as they began to soar and climb through the clouds. Cash attributed the squirmy sensation in his stomach to their ascent instead of watching their dynamics and trying to keep from imagining them in bed together.

Thankfully he was freezing or it might have gotten embarrassing.

"Does that mean you forgive me too?" Sola asked Aarav.

"Absolutely not." He whipped off his seat belt and began pacing before it was probably wise to be unrestrained. Then again it wasn't even the tenth most hazardous thing Cash had seen them do in the brief time he'd known them. "What were you thinking stepping in front of him right then? I could easily have blown your head off!"

So she literally had saved Cash's life. Damn. He wasn't sure if he should be outraged they'd kidnapped him or grateful she'd intervened when he hadn't even known he was at risk.

"Nah. I knew you wouldn't." Sola unclipped too and rose. She crossed to Aarav and laid her hand on his shoulder, massaging the knotted muscles there. "He's a foot taller than me at least and you would have hit him between the eyes. You never miss."

"I was a mile away! If a butterfly farted, I could easily have missed by that much. Besides, even if I'd hit you first it wouldn't have stopped the bullet. I'd just have taken you both out." He pinched the bridge of his nose.

"But you didn't," Sola reminded him.

"I'm going to see that moment in my nightmares for the rest of my life. Your face in my sights." He shuddered then, as if he was the one sopping wet.

"Aarav, it's fine. *I'm* fine." Sola slipped around to his front and Aarav's arms instantly went around her, hugging her tight to his chest despite the wet spot she was undoubtedly leaving all along his front.

They stood there for long enough, rocking slightly with the motions of the jet, that Cash figured he should look away. But he couldn't. They were brave, loyal, and obviously in love.

He was instantaneously jealous. Of a pair of assassins sent to off him.

That was fucked up.

After what seemed like minutes, Aarav release a ragged sigh. "You were right to stop me. Thank you for keeping me from doing something unforgivable."

Sola looked up at him with misty eyes. They leaned closer as if they might kiss, but at the last second, she looked over at Cash instead. "He doesn't deserve to be miserable for the next ten hours. We should let him take a shower and find some dry clothes or give him one of the robes in the bathroom at least."

Aarav cleared his throat and let his hand fall away from her slowly, as if he hated every inch of separation. "Yeah. Okay. Let's get you cleaned up and warm, too."

6

———————

Cash admitted a hot shower sounded like heaven right then. "Thanks. But you're going to have to let my hands free for that. Unless you two plan to join me."

He wouldn't complain if they did. Something good might as well come of all this.

Sola snorted. "Not happening. And you'll have to live with getting naked in front of us. No way am I taking my eyes off you for one second until we figure out what the full story is here. Especially not on a plane over an ocean. Putting myself at risk is one thing, but now you're a wild card for my whole team. If something goes sideways, it's on me."

"Fair enough, I suppose." Cash stood wincing at the squish of his socks.

"That way." Aarav pointed toward the rear of the plane, the only doorway off the main cabin other than the cockpit.

So Cash went. He wasn't surprised to find a luxurious

—if compact—owner's suite, most of which was taken up by a big-ass bed trimmed in some sort of exotic wood. It reminded him a little of his home on his boat, which he was starting to think he might not see again for a while.

He turned away from the sight, almost certain Sola and Aarav had made good use of it on their voyage out to get him and faced the bright white bathroom. He'd never had a problem with baring himself. So when Sola freed his hands, he began to strip.

"Where are your tan lines?" Sola's gaze scanned him from head to toe. Part of her job? Or maybe his attraction to her wasn't exactly one-sided.

"I live on a sailing yacht and spend a lot of time alone at sea. Clothes aren't required when I'm drifting and reading a book." He shrugged.

"Have mercy," she mumbled below her breath.

Aarav shot Cash another glare, but his gaze didn't bounce away nor did it stay fixed on Cash's face. Interesting. Cash smirked.

"You're going to have to wait your turn," Aarav snapped at him. "Sola's going first."

"No." She whipped around toward him. "Don't tell me what to do. I'm fine."

"It only makes sense. This way I can patch you up while he's in the shower and keep an eye on you both." Aarav refused to be swayed.

"I can wait." Cash smiled at her. "Feel better already without those clothes and a gallon of seawater weighing me down."

"This is the weirdest fucking day of my life," she grumbled.

"Same." He couldn't believe it, but he actually chuckled.

"Give me five minutes." She looked between Aarav, his stance wide, arms crossed in his black cargo pants and T-shirt as he hovered over Cash. "You swear you're not going to kill him while I'm in there?"

"Can't now. Jordan won't let me." Aarav deadpanned it, but the corner of his mouth quirked the tiniest bit. Cash figured that was probably about as telling as a full comedy skit performed by someone else.

Sola disappeared into the bathroom. Within seconds, the sound of spray hitting the shower wall was followed by an audible sigh of relief.

"Didn't mean to fuck up your plans for tonight." Cash figured it would be best to get Aarav on his side, or at least less opposed to his presence, if he could.

"Cleaning my gun is fun, but I only do it when necessary." He glanced up at Cash. Was he trying to reassure him he wasn't a cold-blooded killer? That was a hard sell. So Cash returned to lighter subjects, or so he thought.

"Is that what we're calling it these days?" He grinned. "Look, I'd be pissed too if I had intended to spend ten hours in a bed with her on a private jet."

"Don't be thinking of her in bed at all." Aarav practically snarled, so Cash shrugged. They spent the next couple of minutes in absolute silence made no less awkward by the fact that every time his gaze met Aarav's, the other man was ogling some part of his bare body. His Adam's apple, his ass, and even his feet.

He was relieved when Sola opened the door and grabbed a brush to detangle her hair.

She flattened herself to the wall. "Go ahead."

In the tight quarters, Cash still brushed against her as they swapped places. He stepped into the steamy glass enclosure, flipped on the shower, and groaned. The heat was divine seeping into his freezing limbs, yes. But so had been that briefest of contact with the fierce woman who'd spared his life earlier and put him safely in her own harness while she clung precariously to both a stranger and her own existence.

Aarav stood in the entrance to the bathroom. He spoke quietly, as if afraid she would rebuke him again. "Let me help. You're favoring your right arm and I want to take care of your back before you get dressed. Are you hurt anywhere else?"

She hesitated, then shook her head.

Cash soaped himself ten times more slowly than he would have in his boat's head, taking every opportunity to spy on his captors.

"It's not that bad." She shrugged one shoulder over the white towel.

After only a tiny bit of time with them, Cash could have told her that wasn't going to dissuade Aarav from tending to her.

"It is." Cash didn't hesitate to rat her out. "I can see several scrapes clearly from here. You're still bleeding in places and bruises are starting to form."

Aarav bristled, though whether it was because she was injured or because Cash was checking out his woman, Cash couldn't tell and didn't honestly care. Aarav strode into the room and spun her around, slipping the brush from her fingers and working it through the wet strands of her hair carefully until they hung straight to her waist. Then he parted her hair in the center and began braiding it with quick, sure motions of his hands. That meant his knuckles caressed her skin. Sola's eyelids grew heavy as he worked.

Cash took his time lathering his hair, making sure not to get suds in his eyes to obscure the show.

When Aarav moved on to the first aid kit stashed in the medicine cabinet, Sola shot daggers at him in the mirror. "You wouldn't act like this if it had been Liam or Ace who ping-ponged down the cliff. You can't let what happened between us last night change things at work."

Bingo. Cash had known they were lovers. He hadn't realized they were a fresh matchup, though. Cash spread soap over his abs and along his cock. It wasn't his fault if he washed it a few extra times.

"This is exactly why we shouldn't have fucked. Why I resisted it for so damn long. Because you're going to take risks and if you get hurt, I won't be able to handle it." Aarav traced along the edges of the bruises already forming on her shoulder blade, then kissed the area softly before covering it with antibiotic ointment and a bandage.

He adjusted her towel to preserve her modesty, at least on her front side, while opening it in the back. Cash didn't even try to stop himself from staring at her perfect ass. Damn, she was even more built than he'd realized when they were smooshed together. She must spend a hell of a lot of time in the gym.

Sola was impressive and intimidating, a combination his dick liked a tad too much. Especially as Aarav continued tending to her wounds, both of them having forgotten Cash's presence. Aarav caressed her and kissed her, his tender care probably doing as much as the alcohol and ointment to soothe her.

When he'd finished and rewrapped her, Sola spun in his arms, resting her cheek on his shoulder, which was even with hers or maybe an inch lower. "I don't like the thought of you out in the field either. But this is what makes us who we are and what makes us...like...each other."

Cash knew an L word that would have worked better in that sentence.

"I know. It's going to be hard to deal with and we can't let it fuck us up when we're in the thick of things." Aarav did kiss her then. It was long and slow and so damn thorough that Cash knew he'd never really made out with someone the way it should be done before. "I nearly lost it today. You know that never happens. I'm sorry, but James was right. I was terrified that not only might you get hurt, but that I might have been the one to cause your pain."

"Even if you'd pulled the trigger, it would have been me at fault. I deviated from the plan. I just couldn't..." She glanced over at Cash then and realized he was blatantly staring at them, transfixed by the depth of emotion and angst spilling from them.

"You did the right thing," Aarav told her, stroking her jaw. He placed another kiss on her cheek, then followed her gaze.

Which was when he noticed Cash's raging hard-on.

Cash attempted to cover himself with the puny washcloth but it was no use. Was Aarav going to go get his rifle after all? Some guys didn't take kindly to the attention and appreciation of other men.

Surprisingly, Aarav only shook his head. "You're fucked up. Who gets turned on after they've nearly been offed and are taken hostage instead? Do you have a Stockholm Syndrome kink or what?"

Sola whipped her face toward Aarav as if she couldn't believe he'd cracked a joke in those circumstances either. Then she burst out laughing. Was it her dazzling smile or the banking of the jet that knocked him off balance into the shower wall?

Either way, Cash was glad for the assistance in remaining standing.

"I can't help it if my body likes what it sees." He shrugged. Even better, he enjoyed riling up this man, who didn't seem like he often let people get under his skin. "If I was a perv, I'd have jacked off while you made out. Wouldn't have taken much to put me out of my misery."

"You're going to run out of hot water before you get very far." Sola winced. As if on cue, the warmth began to subside, so Cash quickly finished rinsing, then shut off the spray.

Right then a cold shower might have come in handy, but he'd already frozen his balls off enough for one day. Besides, he was suddenly exhausted. Now that he was fairly sure these people had some sort of moral code, and that they weren't about to slit his throat in his sleep when they could have so easily offed him already, he found himself crashing.

"You okay?" Sola asked as she handed him a towel and pointed to a fresh robe hanging on the wall.

"Yeah. I will be. Pretty sure. I was dreading today, having to go to that bullshit ceremony, but I honestly never expected it to turn out like this." Cash turned his back as he dried off, so they wouldn't see his cock was still plenty ready for action. And when he cinched the belt on the robe, he overlapped the panels as far as possible, not that the bulge beneath the fluffy fabric was easy to miss.

"I'm sure the flight crew has meals prepared." Aarav took Sola's gun from his waistband and handed it back to her, reminding Cash that as hot and interesting as they were, they were not people to mess around with. "I'll go get something for us to eat. And then you should try to sleep. Once we land it's going to be...hectic until we get this sorted out."

"Jordan promised he's not going to the basement." Sola stiffened as if she'd fight him over it. Cash knew then, for sure, he was safe with her.

"Even still, there are going to be a lot of questions and a lot to figure out. If you're right, and I'm starting to think you are..." Aarav's eyes blazed. "Then Jordan's going to have a lot of explaining to do. I'm not a weapon to be used without care."

Ouch. Cash wondered what it would be like if Aarav ever truly unleashed himself. He didn't want to be on the receiving end of the man's ire.

Aarav used the food as an excuse to step away, but Cash figured he was not unaffected by whatever was going on between him and Sola, his disappointment in their boss, and whatever the fuck vibe the three of them had going too.

It was complicated, and draining. Although it was barely evening, Cash yawned.

Sola gestured to the bed. "You might as well get comfy. Sorry, but after you eat, I'm going to tie you up again. We don't take chances around here."

"Could have fooled me earlier." Cash wasn't sure he'd ever get the image of her dangling between his legs over hundreds of feet of open air out of his mind. Knowing she'd risked it to save him meant something. He wasn't sure there was anyone in his life who would have done the same besides his mother, and she'd been gone for decades now.

He climbed onto the bed and sat with his back against it.

"Yeah, well, that wasn't typical." Sola surprised him by joining him, stretching her legs beside his. As she rested her shoulders gingerly on the padded headboard, one of her arms touched his. He realized he'd taken up a spot in the middle, leaving room for Aarav on the other side. "And I'm probably going to pay for that for a long time to come. We have to trust each other, completely, on the job or it simply won't work."

"That's true of all relationships, isn't it?" He looked down at her where she toyed with the edge of a matching robe she must have shrugged into when he had his back turned.

"I suppose. Haven't been in many. Okay, none. I mean, unless you count hookups." She winced as she looked up at him then. "Sorry you heard all that between Aarav and me. It's new. We're working on it."

"I got that." Cash wished he could hold her hand. She seemed like she could have used a lifeline herself right then. "I'm sure it will work out. I could see right away you have a connection."

"You could?" Her question came quickly and earnestly. As if she doubted her own perception.

"Yeah." Cash grinned. "He likes you, too."

She laughed and let her head fall back against the headboard. "I hate that I'm so needy and so obvious. What the hell kind of badass agent am I?"

"A pretty damn good one, I'd bet." Cash would have said more, except Aarav returned with a tray loaded with containers.

He stutter-stepped when he saw Sola and Cash sitting on the mattress together.

Sola waved to the empty space on the other side of Cash. "There's only one bed. What you said was right. Tomorrow's going to be a bitch of a day. We need to rest while we can since neither of us slept much last night."

Cash had a pretty good idea of what they'd been doing instead.

"Good thing it's massive, and I'm a sound sleeper." Cash hid his smirk behind his hand, figuring they'd have been plastered on each other for sure without him wedging them apart. "I'm sure you won't even notice me here."

Aarav mumbled something that didn't sound like English beneath his breath and Cash would have bet his father's entire casino it was curse words in his native language. His audible aggravation was both endearing and hot.

Cash turned to Sola and winked. "I see why you like him."

She opened her mouth, maybe to ask if he was into guys, but then shut it as if realizing they weren't actually friends who'd met at the party they'd bailed spectacularly on.

When Aarav passed each of them a meal, all three of them used the excuse to fill their stomachs and occupy their mouths with something other than potentially problematic discussions. And afterward, they were true to their word. Sola bound his wrists and lifted them over his head, hooking them to an eyebolt he hadn't noticed before, embedded in the headboard.

Did they transport fugitives on the jet often? Or was this part of an entirely more enjoyable function of the furniture?

While Sola immobilized his upper body, Aarav cuffed

each of his ankles and secured them to the foot of the bed. Cash had enough leeway to roll from side to side and get mostly comfortable, but no hope of escaping and not enough slack that he could reach either of his babysitters.

Sola and Aarav adjusted their pillows and settled down on either side of him, both of them facing inward, whether to keep an eye on him or to maintain eye contact with each other while he was splayed on his back.

"Can't say as I've ever spent the night strapped to a bed between a sexy woman and her man before, but I'm willing to try anything once." Cash grinned as Aarav squirmed.

It was more fun than he would have guessed to tease the guy. Especially since there was no denying the tent in Aarav's shorts before the guy whipped the covers up to his waist, leaving his spectacular chest and tattooed ribs on display. Damn.

"Shut up and go to sleep," Aarav muttered.

"I guess having a near-death experience makes you pretty aware of the things you've missed out on and might still like to try before you go." He looked to Sola then, who nodded.

"Our jobs make me think about that a lot." She peeked over at Aarav then. Did that bastard know how lucky he was? If not, Cash was more than willing to give Sola whatever she was missing if he could.

There, next to them both, he could sense the difference. They were alive. Fully and truly, where he'd merely been existing until now. Spoiled, rich, and utterly without use to anyone.

It took him a long time, at least an hour after both Aarav and Sola dropped off, to start to doze. In addition to their heat radiating into him, making his entire being buzz, he'd had a lot to think about. If nothing else, that day had taught him that he needed to do more, be better, and try to make a difference so that what he left behind could be superior to what he'd been born into.

He wanted a purpose like theirs, whatever...exactly... that might be.

7

As Aarav held the door to the Shields headquarters open for Cash and Sola with one hand, he reached over his shoulder to rub the back of his neck with the other. His pathetic massage did absolutely nothing to relieve the tension threatening to permanently kink his spine, giving him one hell of a headache. He blinked to clear the black spots that appeared each time he clenched his jaw before reminding himself he needed to relax.

He couldn't decide if he was more frustrated because he hadn't been able to make love to Sola again after her harrowing daredevil escape or because of the churning in his gut that had made it impossible for him to eat a bite of breakfast. That sickness had increased while sharing a bed with Sola and her new pet, especially since each time he'd conked out for a bit he'd had a nightmare about slaughtering someone innocent.

This was exactly why they should never have allowed themselves to give in to the desire that had been brewing between them for months. A couple spectacular hours in the sack had changed his entire life. Part of him couldn't believe it had actually happened. Finally. But the rest was full of condemnation.

Not only was his evolving relationship with Sola screwing with their careers and his ability to be impartial, it had awakened a side of him he'd long kept under control. Or more like, had never had to try to suppress. Before Sola, before his bond with her, he'd never been interested in pursuing a physical relationship with anyone. After a few admittedly stellar orgasms, his body had been on full alert every moment since, including the long flight back with Cash pressed up against one side of him.

He'd vacillated between the horror of bad dreams to jerking awake only to experience his libido reawakening, his cock not getting the memo that his mind was being tortured by what ifs.

What the hell was up with that? It must have been because Sola was so near and yet out of his reach, as she had been all these months. Then he'd lain there restless and horny as hell, until he fell into another fitful slumber.

It had been an entire night of torture that didn't enhance his mood one bit.

Neither did the fact that Sola took Cash's hand as she led him down the hall and into their command center where the rest of the team was already assembled, their usual banter conspicuously absent. No one was happy about this clusterfuck.

When Sola and Aarav dropped into seats at the boardroom table, Cash between them, Jordan cleared his throat and said, "Welcome to Shields. I apologize for the rocky start to things."

"Rocky?" Cash tossed back his head and laughed at

that. "I guess if you're talking about the cliff I had to scale and bashed one of your employees against as she kidnapped me, you'd be right about that."

Jordan winced. "In retrospect, it wasn't done with as much tact as we'd like. But that wasn't exactly the plan."

"No. Excuse me if I'm not in the mood to be cordial since you'd meant for Aarav to blow my fucking brains out." Cash crossed his arms, making the tanned skin of his forearms stretch over corded muscles. Aarav could easily picture him hoisting the sails of his boat in the sunshine and sea breeze. He wasn't meant to be here in this office, half a world away.

"True. But Sola's a hell of an operative and she called him off." Jordan smiled wanly at her then.

"Why did you?" Cash wondered, looking to Sola too.

"It didn't feel right." She shrugged one shoulder and stared at the table directly in front of her instead of meeting anyone's gaze. Aarav hated that he'd played a part in her doubting herself. Never again. Even if that meant becoming uncomfortable and facing whatever the fuck was going on between them, and now Cash—who'd gotten entangled in their bullshit.

"Can you answer some questions for us so we can sort through the intel we have and clear up any misinformation?" Jordan wasn't usually this meek. It only unnerved Aarav more, and yet didn't do much to turn down the flames on the rage bubbling within him.

"Why the hell should I talk to you? Why should I trust any of you?" Cash flung up his hands. "As far as I can tell, you're a fancy bunch of brutes with poor judgment."

Sola winced and shifted away from Cash, who turned toward her and took a deep shaky breath.

"Except for her." He gestured with his thumb at Sola.

"I could remind you that we're armed and prepared to convince you to speak with us however necessary." Jordan didn't back down, because at the end of the day, Cash probably wasn't that far off. If it meant serving the greater good, they were willing to use force. "But we'd much prefer to have a civil conversation."

Sola turned to Cash then, her eyes huge. "Please. Tell them what you know so you can be cleared. If you need protection, we can help you with that too."

"From who?" Cash tipped his head. If he was an actor, he was a hell of a good one.

Jordan drew their attention back to him. He nodded to Ruby, who clicked a few buttons and put up several images on the huge curved screen at the head of the room. They weren't pictures of Cash's dad, though. It was Jay Barber, the arms dealer at the root of the problem. "Do you recognize this man?"

"Yeah." Cash shrugged, but Aarav felt the absolute stillness of every Shield in the room. This moment could change everything. Was he admitting they'd been right at first? "I've seen him with my father once or twice. I try not to be involved, but sometimes he forces me to attend events, like the one yesterday, or he threatens to cut me off."

Cash groaned. "I realize by now I should tell him to fuck off. Yesterday was the last straw. It's more important to me to be left the hell alone. I'll sell my boat. Figure something out. It'll be fine. Better than dealing with his shit."

Aarav's gut twisted at that. It didn't take a master profiler to realize that yacht meant everything to Cash, because it was the place he found peace. He must be serious if he'd consider giving it up.

"Do you know his name? Or what he does for a living?" Jordan kept pushing.

"You really overestimate how many fucks I give about my father's business." Cash shook his head. "If you were hoping I could tell you shit about that, you wasted a hell of a lot of effort, and could have gotten Sola killed."

Aarav wasn't happy about that either. He couldn't think about it too much or the emotions roiling inside him would boil over. He tried to lock them under his usual impassive visage.

"One thing I don't get," Cash continued, "is why some gambling is worth ending someone over. Are you some kind of moral police? Is he cheating or what? I wouldn't put it past him."

That sealed it for Aarav. Because he'd had the same exact question until Jordan had revealed the true underpinnings of the Kalykalaos enterprise.

"He doesn't know shit!" Aarav slapped his palms on the table, drawing the stares of each man and woman around it. Marcus, Kennedy, Knox, Nolan, Ruby, James, Liam, Ace, Tavish, Legend, Ransom, Levi, Sola, and Jordan—every last one of them gaped at him, which only triggered his eruption.

Aarav bolted to his feet, knocking his chair over with a thunderous crash.

He knew he should have taken a walk, found his center, kept his cool, but instead shouts launched from his mouth straight from his soul. It felt so good to get it out, he unleashed his rage, directing it at Jordan. "You damn near made me a murderer. For real. What the fuck?"

His fists balled and he had a vision of launching himself in an epic slide across the polished table to plant his knuckles in Jordan's horrified face, but Sola was there, reaching across Cash, to cover his hands with a gentle squeeze.

Her touch soothed him like nothing else could, encouraging him to take a long, ragged breath and then another until the red haze dissipated and the concern of his friends ringing them penetrated his fury.

James came to the rescue, breaking the edgy silence following the reverberation of his roars. "I've been told we don't use the M word around here, Aarav. But I'm proud of you for expressing your emotions. Seems like it wasn't a wasted trip after all."

Their friends grinned. Ruby winked at Sola, and Kennedy beamed as she leaned her head on Marcus's shoulder.

Jordan cleared his throat. "I'm incredibly sorry, Aarav. And Cash. And Sola. It's my job to make absolutely sure our targets are valid. This will never happen again. I promise you."

Liam, who'd had the misfortune to be sitting on Aarav's other side, rose and picked the chair off the floor, righting it and sliding it back to him. He put his hand on Aarav's shoulder and pressed lightly. "You were doing your job. And you stopped in time. Sola's okay. Cash is okay. You're okay."

Aarav looked down then at Sola and Cash, both of whom were shooting him anxious looks. He allowed his shaky legs to fold then, sinking back into place beside them. He felt an obligation to Cash to protect the man while this got sorted out. He was as blameless as the people who'd been blown up in that market square. The evil they were hunting had nearly cost him his life.

"We will make sure you're safe," Aarav promised him.

"From what?" Cash looked between Sola and Aarav.

Jordan took over, breaking the bad news. "Here's what we had. What I saw…"

Ruby changed the display. Graphic images of Jay Barber, weapons caches, the aftermath in the square, and a pile of documents with Cash's name and supposed signature on them wallpapered the room.

It took a few minutes for Cash to process it all and come to the same conclusion that Jordan had. "My father was going under and he made a deal with those bastards? To what? Launder their money? And he pinned it on me? Jesus fucking Christ!"

"It was a good plan. A great plan even. And very convincing." Jordan winced. "I am truly sorry. For the record, Sola is getting a raise and a hefty bonus for seeing what none of the rest of us did."

"That's not necessary." She shook her head.

Cash put his hand on hers and clasped it, making Aarav jealous…of them both. "I think it's well deserved. If you take it, that will make me feel a lot better about things. It's hard right now for me to have faith in anyone. Except you. And if you vouch for the rest of these people then I'll trust your opinion. In fact, I want to help you put a stop to this. Not only to clear my name, but because this is a new level of disgusting, even for my father."

"You would do that?" Sola asked quietly.

Cash nodded. "I'm well aware he's not a saint. Scruples have never been his thing. I mean, he *is* married to my freaking ex after all, isn't he?"

"That's fucked up." James leaned forward. "I need to know all about it."

Ruby snorted but didn't interrupt Cash as he explained.

"I brought Paris to one of my father's casinos for some

stupid high-roller event. To be fair, I was only really with her to get that asshole off my back. He'd been trying to hook me up with women he approved of every chance he got ever since he walked in on me making out with the son of his head landscaper when I was fifteen." He shrugged, but Sola shifted closer to him, still holding his hand.

Aarav and the rest of the Shields, gauging by their raised brows and glances at where Sola and Cash were linked, would have to be dead not to notice the spark of attraction between them even though they hadn't witnessed Cash's damn impressive erection while watching them from the shower the day before.

It didn't take top-notch investigative skills to figure out Cash was bisexual. If he was waiting for them to be judgmental about it like his father had been, James would be more likely to wear all black first.

"Anyway, I picked someone I knew my father would approve of. I guess I did a little too good of a job." There was no inflection in Cash's explanation, but Aarav knew that strategy well enough. Try to strip out the painful things in life, bury them deep, and act like they didn't matter. It wasn't a viable long-term strategy, as his earlier outburst—and his wild liaison with Sola on the jet —proved.

"So where was his wife yesterday? There were at least a half dozen women drooling over him at the grand opening." Sola cringed.

"Who knows? I said he was married, not faithful." Cash shrugged.

"To be fair, there are an awful lot of people in this room who have multi-partner relationships." James filled Cash in. "I have a wife and a husband. So does Jordan.

Kennedy, Knox, and Marcus are a trio. I could go on but suffice it to say, we understand there are non-traditional arrangements—"

"So you're telling me you're a band of righteous assassins with shoddy informants and kinky sex lives? Good for you. Anyway, that's not what I'm talking about." Cash's easy acceptance made him grow on Aarav a little more. "My father isn't open and honest with Paris about it. His affairs aren't about their mutual desires or consensual exploration. He's just an asshole."

"In that case, fuck him." James glowered.

"Anyway, it's been three years since that whole debacle. During that time, I've kept to myself and he's generally left me alone. It was odd that he insisted I come yesterday and now...I'm wondering..."

"Did his father set this whole thing up?" Sola finished his thought. "Beyond making it look like Cash had done the deal with Jay Barber to cover his own ass, was *Mr. Kalykalaos* trying to get us to off Cash for him and use that as an excuse to cool down on the laundering so he could get back to his life of simple indiscretions without the demands of the gunrunners screwing up his fun?"

"Seems plausible." Jordan steepled his fingers as he considered the possibility. "He certainly has the resources to pay someone off and feed us false data."

"Honestly, this is a new level of scummy, even for him." Cash rubbed his temple.

Aarav understood what it was like for your father to withhold his approval. It was bad enough Cash's father didn't love him, or even like him, but to try to have him killed?

That had to smart.

"It's a slippery slope. He probably only dipped into

laundering to save face and cover his losses. But once you get involved in this kind of shit, there isn't an easy way out." Jordan leaned back in his chair, letting the pause lengthen as he considered what to do next.

"So do I just get on that jet and head back to my boat?" Cash asked wistfully, though he had to know that was impossible.

"No." Aarav, Sola, and Jordan spoke at the same time.

"Sorry. It's obviously not safe." Sola looked up at him.

"Stay here with us. Sola and Aarav will look after you." Jordan eyed the three of them before nodding. "The two of you are neighbors anyway. Move in together and keep an eye on our guest until we can resolve this issue."

Cash opened his mouth as if to argue, but when Sola peered up at him, her big brown eyes practically begging, he made all of their lives easier and gave in. "Okay, but on one condition."

"What's that?" Jordan asked.

"While you're poking around, look into my mother's death. Please. Whenever I would ask about her condition, my father was vague. He said he didn't want to burden a kid with details, but does that really sound like the behavior of the same guy we're talking about here?" Cash flicked his hand at the gory images on the screen.

"No, it doesn't." Jordan sighed.

Cash met Jordan's stare head on. "I want to hear it from you. Tell me what happened to my mom. And if he's responsible, he should pay for it. I want justice for her."

"I'll see if we can get you some answers," Jordan promised. "Hell, maybe it will help us shut him and, ultimately, Jay Barber down for good. Uh, you should be aware, though, that will probably be about the same in the end as you getting cut off. Anything your father earned illegally will be confiscated. A large percentage of his assets will be paid to us as fees. I can't guarantee we'll be able to match what he's giving you, but we'll set you up as best we can to live your life free of all this."

"I don't want my father's dirty money." Cash waved them off. "Wasting it was only fun when I thought it would annoy him. As long as I can keep my yacht, my home, that's all I'm asking for."

Jordan nodded. "Of course."

Around the table, people began to shift in their seats, sensing the meeting was about to be adjourned. So it was obvious when Van and Kyra crawled past the doorway. The blond female drummer for Kason Cox—who happened to be married to Jordan and their wife Wren— and his beefy head of security, whisper-shouted, "Mr. Prickles! Mr. Prickles!"

"What the hell are you two doing?" Jordan asked, making them freeze.

"So sorry. Ignore us." Kyra flashed them an overly bright smile. "*La la la.* We're not listening to the murder meeting details. I swear."

"We do not call them that," Jordan reminded the pair while glaring at James.

"Sure, sure. We're leaving anyway. Unless you've seen Mr. Prickles?" Kyra asked.

"Who?" Cash squinted as he asked Aarav.

"He's their husband Ollie's hedgehog." Aarav couldn't help it—he laughed. What a poor impression they must be making on their protectee. But, then again, this sort of crap was what made them loveable and human and *not* the monsters or killing machines some people would have accused them of being.

Despite their boss's serious expression, James cracked

up. It was his fault the term had caught on after he'd busted in on them planning an operation once, before he'd decided to join them and get them organized.

Cash scanned around the room, finally breaking into a smile of his own.

Kyra dismissed Jordan as she lunged then cursed. "Just missed him. Damn it. We have to get him before Ollie comes home. No one open the outside doors until he's back in his cage."

The pair scurried off in hot pursuit of their husband's pet. Jordan dropped his forehead onto his fist as if regretting mixing their personal and professional lives by having their apartments on the floors above their headquarters. It certainly made things interesting.

But before he could recover from their interruption, a set of keys jingled rhythmically as if someone were flipping them around their finger. The noise got closer until a tall, built man with sandy hair and plenty of tattoos wearing ripped, grease-stained jeans wandered in.

Eli, the owner of the Hot Rods restoration garage, and one of their many friends in Middletown stopped short. "Oh shit. Is this a murder meeting?"

"Don't use the M word!" most of the Shields shouted simultaneously in an attempt to keep Jordan's head from exploding.

"Yeah, right." Eli waved off their objections.

James, however, clutched his stomach and doubled over cackling. He only stopped when Eli launched the keys in his direction. "I brought your car back after those modifications we made."

James snagged them out of the air and bounced up, jogging to the window to look at his miniature green hybrid car. It now resembled some sort of urban warfare tank. If a tank also looked like a booger.

"It's got reinforced steel panels and bulletproof glass." Eli laughed. "Not sure what that's going to do to your mileage, but you should be safe from these idiots backing into you or even the rest of those big ass trees around the parking lot in case there's another storm."

"Perfect!" James clapped, then hugged Eli.

Meanwhile, Aarav stood and stretched, the last of his reservations evaporating. At the end of the day, this was his home and his family. They might have made a mistake, but they weren't evil and they would do their damnedest to make things right.

Cash looked over at Sola then Aarav and shook his head. "This is the most random bunch of people I've ever met. Don't make me regret my decision."

Aarav didn't bother to tell him he hadn't had much choice. They wouldn't have let him leave and risk his life now that they knew what side of the equation he was on. But he allowed the other guy to think it had been a voluntary stay.

"Come on. We'll show you around and introduce you to all these weirdos." Sola grinned as she took one each of Cash's and Aarav's hands and tugged them toward the crowd.

8

———

Sola couldn't fully explain the anticipation racing through her as she showed Cash the parts of her life at Shields that made the place so much more than simply where she worked. At least partially it had to do with Aarav being by her side, knowing they were going to be living together for a while. Not across the hall from each other. Not pretending they were merely friends.

But maybe, finally, exploring what they could be to each other if they allowed themselves to take the risk. And with Cash in the mix...

She kept playing over the facts he'd relayed, even if they weren't for the purpose her mind was putting them to now. He was bi. He obviously had liked what he'd seen in the plane bathroom the night before, and his jokes about being tied to the bed between her and Aarav took on an entirely new spin now that she knew he wasn't opposed to either of them or being open-minded about the various flavors attraction could come in.

Maybe what she was feeling was relief. A lessening of the guilt weighing her down. She'd so recently gotten exactly what she'd been craving for months when Aarav had let her be his first lover, only to suddenly be moved by an instant and potent connection to a man who wasn't her partner. Holy shit.

Was this how Kennedy had felt when she'd clung to her love for Knox, her childhood sweetheart, while also embracing her newer devotion to their fellow Shield, Marcus?

She bet it was. But what was Aarav thinking?

Hell, it had taken her damn near a year to get him to even consider sleeping with her. Now that his walls were down, would he allow her in deeper or would Cash's presence reset the progress they'd so recently made?

"Wow, you've thought of everything, haven't you?" Cash seemed suitably impressed given how he'd grown up. "It's like you have the necessities without any of the waste. Nothing is simply for show, is it?"

"Nah, that's not our style." Aarav glanced around the gym. An indoor track circled a rock-climbing wall and more weights and machines than the local fitness center had. Beyond it was the pool area where Tavish and Legend dove in to do a million and a half laps as usual.

"The stripper pole is a nice touch." Cash seemed suitably impressed as Laurel worked through her routine.

Sola tapped him in the gut with the back of her hand. "I don't blame you for gawking. That's Laurel. She used to be a professional and prefers to keep in shape by dancing. She's been teaching Ruby and the rest of us some tricks. We're nowhere near as good as her, but James is picking it up the fastest so far. Guess it runs in the family. They're siblings."

"Feel free to show me your routine sometime." Cash grinned, risking Aarav doing more than just tapping him.

"Not likely." Sola glanced away, still unused to such blatant attention given Aarav's usual distance.

"Why not? You're beautiful when you dance." Aarav nearly knocked her on her ass when he spoke up, maybe to make Cash envious. No matter, she would take the compliment. "Beautiful *and* powerful. That takes a lot of strength and grace."

"Thank you," Sola said as she met his stare.

"Plus it makes for good scenery when we're working out." He flashed one of his rare and slightly wicked grins. "I've lost count of how many times Ace and Liam have dropped their weights on their toes when they couldn't take their eyes off Ruby. Never gets old."

Cash laughed along with Aarav at that. "I bet. So does everyone in this place hook up or what?"

"It seems that way lately." Aarav surprised her with his honesty. "It's a little hard to be around so many blissful couples, or trios, or whatever you call James and his Powertools—they're a construction crew and also get it on sometimes—when you're not in a relationship yourself. Maybe it's seeing so many people be that ridiculously happy that convinces you it's a good idea, or maybe we're all drawn to each other because of our common beliefs, but it does seem like Middletown is a matchmaking hotbed."

"Maybe its magic can rub off on me." Cash stared off into the distance before clearing his throat. "Uh, is there a kitchen around here? I'm starving."

"Of course." Sola guided him down the hall toward the giant communal cooking and eating space where they often gathered together for meals even though they each had their own facilities in their generous and well-appointed living areas upstairs. "Sorry, I know it's been like twelve hours since we ate."

"I didn't have much of an appetite before." Cash cleared his throat. "But I'm feeling better about things now. I'm probably an idiot for saying this but...seeing you all together. That you have standards and morals, well, I think you're probably the most respectable people I've ever known. Even if you are...you know...the M word I'm not supposed to say."

"You're catching on quick, newcomer," Sevan teased from where she sat between her husbands, Ransom and Levi.

"Thanks." Cash held out his hand to her and then her guys, introducing himself officially.

"We're about to make a few plates. There's some leftover chicken and stuff to whip together a salad. Want to help?" Levi offered as they drew Cash aside.

"Yeah sure. Thanks." Cash looked over at Sola, then went along when she didn't object.

Sola didn't try to eavesdrop when Sevan lowered her voice, figuring she was sharing something personal given how she could relate to Cash. After all, her own stepfather had been the president of an outlaw motorcycle gang that she'd gone undercover to stop. Sola backed up a bit, giving them space.

Aarav wandered to the cabinet where he kept a stash of his precious tea and all the related accessories he required to brew a perfect cup.

"Hey, come chat a second." James patted the bench beside his spot at the long table that could easily seat an army.

Sola sank beside him, across from their medic,

Kennedy, and Ruby—her two closest friends—who were also giving her curious stares. "What's up?"

"First of all, how are you?" he asked.

"Fine. My back is sore, and I think I just about dislocated my arm, but it'll be good as new in a few days. Cash was being a bit dramatic before. It wasn't that bad." She neglected to discuss how she'd clung to him for dear life, praying her dress would hold if her sweaty fingers slipped even a fraction of an inch.

"I'm glad to hear it, and Kennedy will verify before too long, I'm sure, but that's not what I meant." James stared at her, giving her the don't-act-dumb look he should patent. "You and Aarav. It happened, didn't it?"

"Yup." She nodded, peeking over at Aarav being adorable, measuring out his loose leaf and sugar so damn precisely. Setting his milk off to the side, just so.

"I could tell immediately." James grinned. "He's so...*emotional.* I mean, for him. Did you see how pissed he got at Jordan and how he let it out? You're good for him, Sola."

"I don't know about that." She bit her lip. "Uh, I don't want to spill his personal business..."

"Girl, every single person who works here watched Knox fuck me on assignment that one time." Kennedy talked with her hands, trying to convey how absurd she thought Sola was being. "We've walked in on half the people here screwing in the hot tub at some point or other and heard most of the rest. It's not like we have a lot of secrets around here."

"I'll help. Just nod if I'm right." James jumped in. "He was a virgin, wasn't he?"

Sola bit her lip. She needed advice. These people

loved them both and would try to steer her in the right direction. So she nodded.

"I'm sure you rocked his world." Ruby smiled, apparently happy for both of them.

"You know why, don't you?" James leaned in closer.

"He told me he's demisexual. I generally get that, but I haven't had a chance to read up and fully understand the intricacies of what that means." She met James's curious gaze. "Can you give me the rundown?"

"Of course. Because I don't want either of you to accidentally get hurt. It means, by default, Aarav's feelings are involved. Otherwise he wouldn't be attracted to you."

"Oh. Are you sure?" He'd told her as much, but that wasn't what was confusing her.

"Positive. So be careful with him," James advised. "He's not capable of fucking just to get off or to have a good time, even if you are."

"Okay, but then..."

"What?" Kennedy wondered, her concerned stare raking Sola's face.

"Why does it seem like there's this...energy...between me, him, and Cash?" Sola was honest. "From the moment I saw him in that casino, I felt it. And last night..."

"What about it?" Ruby took a gulp of her ice water as if she needed to cool down at the thought alone.

"I mean, nothing tangible. Not really. We didn't have some kind of threeway or something, but let's just say, Cash is clearly not turned off by us. He, uh, was pretty obvious about that. And it didn't seem to freak Aarav out like being around me has these past several months. So what the fuck does that mean?"

"It might mean you've gotten as lucky as the rest of these fuckers," Ruby grumbled.

"You could too if you invited Ace and Liam over to watch a movie and made it a porn instead of a thriller. I bet it wouldn't take much." Kennedy rolled her eyes at Ruby.

"Yeah, right. They're into each other, pretty sure. But that's it. Anyway, we're talking about Sola…"

"Here's the thing." James was uncharacteristically serious for a moment. "Being demi just means there has to be some kind of emotional bond. It doesn't mean undying love or the forever and always sort of commitment. Maybe he can sense whatever is there between you and Cash and it makes it okay for him too."

"Huh." Sola pressed her hand to her face, hoping she wasn't as red as she imagined.

"So if you're thinking you might like to try what so many of us here can promise you is incredible with the right people," Kennedy added, speaking as both her friend and her physician. "Maybe you should give it a try as long as you tread carefully."

"As if this thing with Aarav wasn't full of enough landmines." Sola grimaced. "I have this horrible feeling that if I put one foot wrong I could blow everything up. And if that's the case, I'm happy to work on what's between us before I go and fuck it all up before it's hardly gotten started."

"Whatever happens, you know we're here for you." Ruby set her glass down a little too hard. "Even if you turn out to be one of the lucky bitches around this place."

"Hey, us lucky bitches are hoping for the same for you." James tapped his glass against hers.

Before Sola could thank her friends for grounding her and convincing her she wasn't turning into a raging nymphomaniac, Cash shouted.

She spun around fast enough to make her back protest, calling her a liar for her previous brushoff. Kennedy narrowed her eyes, but Sola didn't wait for a lecture—she jogged over to Cash but relaxed when she realized he was cradling a squirming spiky ball with tiny black eyes and a pointy nose against his chest.

Her heart melted when he triumphantly declared, "Got him! Sorry to inform you Mr. Prickles ate most of the salad while you weren't looking, though."

"Aw, isn't he adorable?" Sola edged closer so she could pet him with the tip of one finger. "I've never had a pet before."

"Me either," Cash admitted.

"Or me," Aarav said.

"I always thought a bunny would be perfect, but maybe I should have considered a hedgehog." Sola watched his whiskers bobbing from up close as he swallowed the last of their salad.

"Hey, nice work!" Sevan patted Cash's shoulder as Kyra and Van bolted into the room.

"Mr. Prickles, don't you dare take off like that again. Ollie would be crushed if something happened to you." Kyra held out her hands and Cash handed him over to her. She and Van disappeared down the hall toward the elevator to their private quarters.

Cash seemed pretty proud of himself as the Shields congratulated him on his rescue, making Sola warm and floaty inside. She glanced over at Aarav, who seemed awfully content, leaning up against the counter next to his steeping tea. "One more minute and we can head upstairs. Wren promised me she stocked my fridge with plenty of leftovers from the reception."

"You have some of that black cherry cake still?" Nolan

lifted his head so quickly he looked more like a prairie dog with excellent hair than an assassin.

Sola choked as she remembered last time she'd had some, licked off of Aarav's skin.

Aarav grinned at her. "Sure do. But you can't have it. I need it."

Sola was sure now that her cheeks were flaming. Cash nudged her shoulder. "Was it that good?"

"It was incredible." She breathed out a sigh and all their friends—not stupid and no strangers to good sex—cracked up.

Aarav glanced at his wrist again, unwilling to ruin his tea, not even for an epic orgasm or five.

"Dude, if you're as loaded as I'm guessing considering how much Jordan must be paying you to do his dirty work, you can spring for a new one of those," Cash teased as he pointed at Aarav's scratched and dented watch.

Everyone went quiet. Because they knew it meant much more than a way to keep time to him. "It was my father's. I got it off his body when they pulled it from the rubble of a collapsed building after an earthquake. Not everything has to be fancy or expensive to be valuable, Cash."

"Oh. Shit. I was only joking." Cash put his hand on Aarav's shoulder. "Believe me, I've had plenty of spare change in my life, and none of it bought me a father whose watch I'd keep if something happened to him."

Aarav nodded, though he didn't take his stare from his teacup. He blew across the surface, then took a sip though it had to be scalding. Maybe it helped distract him from memories so painful he had never talked much about them to any of the Shields, Sola included.

"I'll do my best to remember I'm not really one of you

and keep my mouth shut from now on." Cash blew out a breath that ruffled his dark hair before turning away.

"It's fine. No big deal." Aarav picked up his tea and walked from the room without turning to see if Cash or Sola were following, though they were.

Sola reached out and claimed Cash's hand, letting him know he was forgiven, at least by her. "Come on. Let's get you something to eat."

"I might have lost my appetite again," Cash muttered, though he didn't balk or refuse to go with them unless they threatened him at gunpoint. So that was progress, at least.

Her life was so fucked up that being a killer for hire didn't even rank in her top three issues.

9

———

Cash swallowed a huge bite of the meal Sola had warmed up for him and hummed. It could have been a TV dinner and it would have rivaled the best gourmet meals he'd ever eaten, but it was honestly impressive. Steak with a red wine demi-glace, steamed vegetables with some kind of buttery sauce that melted on his tongue, and fresh bread with a crusty outside and a soft inside.

He practically inhaled it.

In the background, the shower splattered. Aarav had insisted he'd rather wash off than eat with them. Cash figured the guy needed a minute to himself and he didn't blame him after all they'd been through and the bad memories Cash had inadvertently brought to the surface.

"A couple of our friends—Devra and Morgan—own a restaurant and bakery down the street. Their food is always incredible, but they really took things up a level for the wedding reception." Sola's wistful smile made Cash realize how much the celebration had meant to her.

"Sorry you had to leave early because of the situation with my father."

"It's my job." She shrugged. "Besides, as wild as it's been, I wouldn't change the last couple days for anything. A lot of good has come of it too. You're in one piece and protected here. And, well, stuff with Aarav is...progressing."

"Is that what you call it when you fuck someone halfway across an ocean?" Cash chuckled as he dug into another forkful.

But Sola didn't laugh. Instead, she shifted in her seat. "I don't know if we should talk about that. Not when everything is so fresh and there's this energy zipping around right now."

"Is that what you call this?" He wiggled his fork between them. Then between himself and the general direction of the bathroom. "And this?"

"You feel it too?"

"I'm not dead, am I?" He grunted. "Bad choice of words."

She looked up at him and laughed at his morbid humor. He figured that was a requirement of her occupation.

"Look, just because we have some kind of vibe going on doesn't mean we need to act on it. I'm not trying to screw up your relationship, or whatever it is you have with Aarav. Seems like it was a long time coming."

She nodded. "It was. More than six months of torture. Being best friends, hanging out, working together, hitting the gym, cooking dinner..."

"So, basically, dating but without the sex." Cash winced. "That sucks."

"Yeah, exactly. But there was definitely no suckage."

She ran one hand down her braid before gnawing on a roll without eating more than a crumb. "And now that we did it, we never really got a chance to process what happened and things are awkward and I have no idea how he feels about any of this. About me."

"It was obvious from the moment he stepped into that powerboat that he loves you and would do anything to defend you." Cash couldn't believe she didn't know it too. "Sometimes guys aren't trying to be malicious, they're oblivious. Or in denial. I mean, I didn't even realize what my dad was up to right in front of my face."

"Don't beat yourself up about that. It's hard to be honest about your parents' shortcomings even when they've made huge mistakes in the past." She dropped the roll on her plate.

"Sounds like you've had personal experience. I'm sorry." He didn't press, though he was curious. She took a big glug of water then unloaded on him.

"My dad died in a car accident when I was seven. He was coming home from working third shift and a drunk driver hit him head on. My mother never forgave herself since she had been a stay-at-home mom after having me and he was always struggling to make ends meet for us. She got depressed, was hooked on prescription drugs on and off for years. Finally got sober for good around the time I was in my senior year of high school. Or at least I thought. One night she borrowed my beater, said she had a craving for some chocolate. It was a craving, all right. After being clean nearly a year, she overestimated her tolerance and OD'd before I could track her down when she'd been gone to the 'store' for far too long."

Cash set his fork down, wiped his face on the cloth napkin Aarav had set beside his plate, then took her trembling hand in his. "You're not responsible for her decisions."

"No, but like you said...I wanted to believe it was finally and truly over. Well, in a way, I guess it was." She looked up at him, her warm eyes swimming with emotion. "I've been on my own ever since. Realistically from the day my dad died and I ended up taking care of my mom the best I could. Until I came here. Until I met Aarav and the rest of the Shields. Until they took me in and made me part of their family. Which is pretty damn good, but not entirely what I need. Maybe all I really want is to not be alone anymore."

Her wish struck Cash square in the chest. He'd often had the same thoughts as he bobbed around at sea, literally adrift—in life and in love. He'd seen an echo of the same loneliness in Aarav's expression when he'd talked of losing his father, and likely the rest of his family.

No wonder they understood each other so well.

Despite what he'd said before, he wasn't about to leave her exposed and vulnerable when she'd just admitted she craved someone by her side. Cash leaned in and put his hand on the side of her face, pulling her toward him.

She didn't flinch or retreat. Instead she met him halfway.

Their lips were nearly touching when Aarav walked in, a towel over his head as he mopped the water from his hair and where it dripped onto his bare shoulders and hewn chest. Both Sola and Cash jerked apart so hard their chairs scraped across the tile, drawing his attention.

Sola bolted to her feet, her hands out. "Nothing happened."

But it had been about to. Cash couldn't do anything

but stare and hope he hadn't done the one thing he'd said he wouldn't.

Annoyance knitted Aarav's thick brows. "Do you think I can't see you're attracted to him? Well, welcome to the fucking club. So am I. I think. Even though we just met. Which is really fucking weird because that *never* happens to me. Or maybe I'm extra horny after being around you and knowing how I feel and what we did and it's rubbing off on him."

To be honest, Cash was fine with any rubbing off these two did on him.

"Although that was probably a waste of a cold shower." Cash didn't have to be a super spy to detect the bulge in Aarav's gray sweatpants. Was the man trying to drive him and Sola mad? "I don't own you, Sola. Don't feel obligated to be exclusive with me because we fucked once and my sex drive has some sort of sick and twisted sense of humor."

"I'm sorry." She looked at one man then the other from her place between them, and Cash had no idea what she was apologizing for. For her obvious and longstanding desire for her partner, or because she'd been eyeing Cash like a juicy sausage from the moment they'd met?

Either one didn't feel worth an anguished apology to him.

"I'm ruining everything." Sola sliced her hands through the air. "I'm afraid of starting something with you if I'm not sure it's going to be forever given that we work together and knowing that you're only into me because you have feelings. It's a big responsibility."

Oof. Not how a man wanted a woman to feel about a relationship with them. That it was some kind of burden.

Cash winced and wondered if he should intervene before they unintentionally upset each other more.

He didn't, staying out of their business as much as possible for a man locked in with them.

"You're going to change your mind now?" Aarav scrubbed his hands over his face. "I'm not saying you shouldn't, if that's how you feel. Of course you should. It's just...frustrating, because for months you've been giving me the green light and losing patience and now that I've gone for it, taken the leap despite how fucking terrifying all this is, you're pulling back."

"I'm not rejecting you." Sola laid her hand on Aarav's forearm. "I'm confused."

"Is it because you know that I've never been with anyone else or felt this way before you? And now maybe him." Aarav swallowed hard as if his body had betrayed him.

Wait. What?

Cash nearly toppled out of his chair. Was Aarav saying what he thought?

Not that he'd never been in love before, because certainly he couldn't have that kind of emotion for someone he'd barely met, but that he'd never experienced attraction, passion...or even sex?

Had Aarav been a virgin before that fateful trip? No wonder these two were so on edge around each other. Cash thought back to the way he'd teased them the night before in the shower and then on the bed between them like a human cock blocker. It had been amusing to him, but for them...it must have been torture.

Oh shit. How could he help? How could he repay some of the risks they'd taken for him and for each other?

"Hey, if it helps, this doesn't have to be an existential

crisis. You two are hot as hell and I'm obviously into you both. We're adults. So what's the big fucking deal if we spend some of our time together making each other feel good? Maybe it will lower the stakes some if we simply acknowledge it and get it out of our systems."

"With anyone else, you'd probably have it right." Aarav groaned. "You don't get it. *Getting it out of my system* isn't a thing for me. I've never gotten turned on like this before. It's new and kind of screws with my head."

"Because I'm a guy?" Cash tipped his head, trying not to take it personally.

"Kind of, but not exactly." Aarav took a few long deep breaths as if to physically calm himself down. Sola went to him and wrapped him in a hug. He clutched her as tightly as she'd done to Cash when dangling over the ocean. "More because it doesn't happen with anyone. I'd never even considered it might with a guy. Though after coming to Shields and seeing how content our friends are in their non-traditional relationships, I wouldn't have objected. It's new. It's scary. And there's a lot at stake if I get it wrong."

He peered at Sola, then kissed her softly, as if the taste of her lips reassured him.

Cash couldn't look away. Nor could he deny that he wanted to share in whatever potent thing was blossoming between them.

"Having sex with you must have broken me," Aarav whispered against Sola's lips. "Because now that's all I want. Even if it means sharing you with him."

"I hate to break it to you...but it sounds to me like she fixed you," Cash murmured.

"No, there was nothing wrong with him to begin with and there's not now." The flecks of gold around Sola's irises shone as she argued with Cash. "It's not like I have a magic pussy. Aarav, maybe you're just more receptive to these feelings when you have some kind of bond with someone. Maybe it's safer if you think you won't lose them after what happened to your family and how they were taken from you."

That made a lot of sense to Cash. He didn't particularly like the idea of finding people who both understood him and turned him on only to have them ripped away again. "I could see that."

"There's obviously something here." Sola stepped back so she could look at both of them at once. "I don't want to ignore it and end up regretting it for the rest of my life."

Cash didn't dare speak. He waited for Aarav to make up his mind. When the other man nodded slightly, something inside him shifted and he prayed things were about to go down like he imagined they would.

Aarav said, "I can get behind that. When I watched everything at the casino going down yesterday, the only thing I could think was that I might have missed my chance to tell you how important you are to me and that all I want to do, for the rest of my life, is try to make you as happy as it makes me to spend time with you."

Sola put her fingers over her parted lips, but they didn't fully stifle her gasp. "I love you too, Aarav."

He crushed his mouth to hers then, making Cash envious of them both. If nothing else, they'd have each other. And maybe, if he was lucky, he might get to share a taste of what that kind of link was like. Even if only for one night.

"And because I love you, Sola, I want you to have everything you desire. Including him." Aarav pointed to

Cash. "He'll probably do a hell of a lot better job than I could of satisfying you with absolutely no experience."

Sola snapped, "I enjoyed it plenty. Couldn't you tell? Are you really *that* clueless?"

"Yes. Yes, I am. Didn't I just say that?" Aarav huffed out a self-deprecating laugh. "I'm so far out of my league, it's ridiculous. Especially considering the disproportionate population of sexperts in this town. Hell, in this very building."

"Well, you're in luck." Cash grinned wide and slow. "Because I'm more than willing to teach you everything I know."

Aarav had no idea how they'd arrived at this place he wouldn't even have been able to imagine two days ago, but he couldn't say he was sad that they were there. He led the way into his bedroom, dragging Sola, who in turn towed Cash behind her.

All he knew was that he'd been lucky enough for her to share herself with him once already and didn't seem too upset by the idea of doing it again. This time with reinforcements.

As weird as it was to consider having an audience—and a few extra helping hands—when he had hardly gotten used to the way his senses intensified around Sola, Aarav couldn't deny it took some of the pressure off to have someone more skilled as backup. Because the absolute worst-case scenario would be if Sola didn't get everything she needed from the experience, especially after being so patient and waiting so long for him to get over his hang-ups.

He wanted to show her exactly how much she meant

to him, and having Cash there would ensure he could do that. If there was some additional part of him that liked the idea of the other guy watching and participating, and maybe of...more...between them, then it had to be because what worked for Sola worked for him too.

At least that's what he was telling himself as he made quick work of the sweats he'd only tugged on minutes ago, the waistband pressing his cock down so that when the pressure was released it bobbed and swayed, heavy between his legs.

"Damn." Sola licked her lips and reached for him.

"I can understand your eagerness. But not yet." Cash held her shoulders to keep her from claiming her prize.

Taking his cue, Aarav stepped back, his dick jerking in protest. Cash dipped his head, kissing Sola's neck from behind, making her eyes flutter closed. Aarav braced himself for a wave of jealousy that never came. It only aroused him further to see her enjoy herself, surrendering to this new and strengthening bond between them.

"Come undress her. Slowly," Cash instructed.

Aarav nodded. He wanted to savor the moment and make memories he'd never forget. Sure, he'd enjoyed the frantic coming together they'd had last time, but now...he aimed for at least some finesse. So instead of rending her clothes and stripping her bare in seconds flat, he started with her hair.

He took the elastic from the end of her braid and began to loosen it, unweaving the strands until they hung around her in curtains of soft waves. Then he massaged her head, making her moan and relax backward against the support of Cash's chest.

Aarav couldn't stop himself from sipping from her lips before placing reverent kisses on her cheeks and over her eyes. The room was hushed, the only sound that of their breathing, which started to synchronize as they came together.

He rested his forehead on hers as his hands trailed down her arms, briefly holding her hands before shifting to the hem of her shirt. He lifted it, Cash raising her arms so Aarav could drag the soft material over her torso before folding it neatly and placing it on a nearby chair.

"This is going to be so good," Cash whispered in Sola's ear, making her sigh. "Watch him. See how desperate Aarav is to have you and how much control he has."

"Too damn much," Sola grumbled, but she looked. And when their gazes collided, he swore his cock got even harder.

Her stare tracked his hands as he gripped her waist then sank to his knees, trailing the tip of his tongue along the ridges of her abdomen while his fingers dipped, sliding inside the waistband of her yoga pants. He peeled them down her sculpted legs, admiring every inch of muscle and the hard work she'd put in to turn her body into the marvelous machine it was.

Cash wrapped his arms around her midsection and lifted, so Aarav could slip her pants and socks from her feet. He stood gradually, adding the rest of her clothes to the neat pile he'd started before.

Now only her underwear and Cash's say-so separated them.

"Don't rush," Cash told Aarav. "Take your time to look. Really see all of her. She's making herself vulnerable and I guarantee she doesn't do that with just anyone. If you appreciate her mind as well as her body, you'll be a far better lover."

Sola shivered at that. Then she griped, "I'm changing my decision. Cash is a bad influence on you."

Cash chuckled. "If that's really true, I'll go and leave you two to this."

Sola clutched his arm where it rested beneath her breasts. "Don't you dare or I'll let Aarav shoot you next time."

He only laughed harder, inspiring Aarav to grin in return. Still, he didn't shirk the duties Cash had given him. Not when they were such enjoyable tasks anyway. He stood back far enough to let his gaze roam over Sola, not only from her pussy, which was forming a damp spot on her panties or the beaded tips of her breasts surging against her bra, but the way she'd gone pliant. Letting Cash hold her, steady her, while Aarav got her ready for them.

It wasn't natural for her to submit, and yet it seemed effortless in these circumstances. "Thank you for sharing this with me. You're gorgeous, Sola. And so brave."

Aarav's praise only seemed to heighten her arousal. She shifted her feet, unconsciously widening her stance, making it easy for him to press his palm to her mound and cup her humid flesh. She ground against him, mewling as he provided a hint of relief that was accompanied by the tease of more to come.

When he withdrew, her hips chased after his touch, but he shifted his attention to her shoulders instead, nudging the straps of her bra off her freckled shoulders, kissing the skin where they'd been.

"That's good, Aarav. Nice and slow. Savor it." Cash's instructions seemed more gravelly than only moments before. Maybe because Sola was rubbing against him, her ass cradling his cock, which Aarav would bet his entire life savings was as hard as his own.

Aarav continued kissing and licking along the edge of the red lace bra cupping her breasts. Getting drunk on the baby powder scent of her soft skin. He reached around behind her, his fingers rubbing Cash's chest in the process, making the other man suck in a sharp breath.

Oh, he could get used to this. Aarav glanced up and smiled wickedly.

"You have no idea what kind of fuck monster you've created." Sola groaned and shuddered between them.

"I'm starting to have a clue." Cash didn't seem too upset about it either. "Go ahead, Aarav. Take it off her. Show us her tits."

Ordinarily he would have objected to such crude language, but in the heat of their exchange it didn't seem to bother Sola and only urged Aarav on. So he did. He peeled the satin and lace from her, watching her breasts bounce as they were set free.

They weren't unobstructed for long, though, as his head dipped so he could suck on first one then the other while Cash told them both how sexy it was to watch Aarav feasting on her.

Sola moaned and hiked one thigh over Aarav's hip, as if trying to align her core with his hard-on. Now that he'd gotten a taste for this game, there was no way he was going to let either of them off the hook so easily. This was pleasure and pain wrapped in one and he intended to prolong it until neither of them could bear it any more.

Cash shifted his hand, cupping one of Sola's breasts as Aarav experimented with kisses, sucks, the scrape of teeth, and even light bites on the other. She arched in his hold, her head going back onto his shoulder. He leaned down and brushed his lips over hers. Sola strained toward them both, her mouth seeking Cash's as her body sought Aarav's.

He let his hands wander across all of her, petting and caressing her as he drew on her nipples. And when his fingers landed on her panties, his hands clenched the material, causing the snap of threads to overlay their ragged breathing.

"That's one way." Cash stopped kissing Sola long enough to check on Aarav's progress. "You could rip them off her, but they're awfully pretty."

Aarav was thankful the other man was there to keep him in check and help him make this as thrilling as possible for Sola. At the end of the day, he cared about her pleasure far more than his own. He eased his grip, instead nudging the material down her thighs until they dropped away.

"Good." Cash nodded at Aarav. "Since you're already naked, get on the bed."

He felt somewhat self-conscious crawling onto the mattress, but also empowered. This was who he was, bare and raw. If they liked what they saw, they accepted all of him. Judging by Cash's slap on his ass, the soft, hungry noises Sola made as Cash handed her to him, and the obvious tent in the other guy's pants, there was no doubt he was doing this right.

"Entertain her while I strip too." Cash put his hands on the back of Sola and Aarav's heads and guided them together.

Aarav didn't have to be told twice. He cradled Sola sideways in his lap, wrapping her in his arms as the outside of her thigh pressed against the full length of his cock. It pulsed. Precome dampened the tip, causing him to wonder precisely how long Cash was going to be able to keep them apart.

Aarav stared into Sola's eyes as she settled in for a long, sweet kiss. She nipped his bottom lip between her teeth before slipping her tongue into his mouth and parrying with his.

His hands roamed her back and side until Cash drew their attention. He was towering over them at the side of the bed, his hand stroking his impressive cock from root to tip ever so slowly. "Did you know it can take forty-five minutes for a woman's internal genitals to become fully aroused? They fill with blood and change shape, making penetration more pleasurable for both her and her partner."

"I'm fully fucking aroused right now." Sola dug her nails into Aarav's shoulder as if that tiny discomfort would convince him to rush instead of spurring him to continue down this very long and winding road to ecstasy. "In fact, I'm wound up so tight I might break something if I don't come soon."

"I didn't say we weren't going to make you orgasm before then, but no one will be fucking you until you're completely ready." Cash crawled toward them. He tugged Sola's hair, exposing her neck to Aarav, who didn't hesitate to kiss the apparently sensitive spot beneath her ear. "Beg all you want, I like to hear it. But it's not going to change my mind. Or Aarav's. Right?"

He might die first, but he wasn't putting his dick anywhere near her pussy until Cash told him he should. "Right."

"Damn you both." Sola drummed her heels on the bed. "Two incredible cocks right here and you won't give them to me?"

"Not yet." Cash stroked her cheek before pressing his thumb to her lips. She parted them and sucked it inside as if doing so soothed some of her aching neediness. "Come here, Aarav."

He reluctantly set Sola against the pile of pillows he'd considered a waste when James had picked them out. The guy had not only designed the building and overseen its construction, but also teamed up with Kate and Laurel, who owned a refurbished home furnishings company, to decorate most of the spaces too. He'd have to remember to thank them later.

Much later.

Aarav scooted around to sit on his haunches next to Cash at her feet.

"Do you see what you do to us?" Cash asked Sola before shocking the hell out of Aarav by reaching over and encircling his cock. "Look at this. You did this. To him. And to me."

Cash took Aarav's closest hand and drew it to his own shaft. The other man's erection felt heavy and thick as Aarav's fingers curled around it. They stayed there, rubbing each other's dripping dicks as Sola admired them. One of her hands wandered to her chest while the other snaked between her legs.

She sighed and parted them as her fingertip circled her engorged clit.

"Why don't you do that for her?" Cash fisted his hand in Aarav's hair and used the grip to lower Aarav's head toward Sola, who spread her thighs to make room. "But with your tongue. Make it flat when you lap at her slit and pointed when you run it around her clit. Go ahead. Have a taste."

Another sharp spank echoed through Aarav's

bedroom and the burn in his ass only amplified his desire. He was afraid he might shoot as soon as his dick touched the sheets, never mind Sola's pussy. Cash had better know what he was doing.

At least if Aarav ruined the fun, the other man would be there to finish the job for him.

He couldn't wait to feel Sola's wetness slicking his beard as it had the other day. This time he was going to savor it as she rode his face and her thighs hugged his shoulders. The first flavor of her on his taste buds made him groan and he tucked his mouth tighter to her core.

Her hands flew to his shoulders, her nails scratching them lightly in rhythmic arcs that showed him exactly how she wanted him to work his tongue against her. Meanwhile, Cash climbed higher on the bed, his body lying along Aarav's while he massaged, kissed, and kneaded Sola from the waist upward. They made out as Aarav feasted on her, abiding by Cash's periodic orders.

A long time later, when Sola was gasping with each brush of his lips over her clit, Cash turned to Aarav. "Give her a finger. Just one. To hold while you take her over this first time."

"More." Sola squirmed beneath them. "Fuck me. Please!"

"Ah, there. I told you I love it when you cry out for us. But no. Not yet. He will make you come, though. Show him how good he's doing between those fine legs." Cash caressed her cheek, then looked to Aarav. "Palm facing the ceiling, curl your finger upward and press near her pubic bone. She'll fly apart as soon as you find the right spot."

Aarav nodded, then pressed his middle finger to her opening, which was much slicker and puffier than it had been on the jet. He hoped that didn't mean he'd hurt her that night, though she hadn't seemed in the least uncomfortable. Now that he knew better, he intended to do better.

Aarav did as Cash told him. He fed Sola his finger, groaning as her pussy clasped it tight and drew it deeper. He twisted his wrist so his hand aligned in the proper direction, then curled his finger in a come-hither motion. He tried it once, twice, three times before he met some resistance against her pelvis.

Sola screamed his name and shattered, hugging Cash to her as she did.

They made out as Aarav followed the bucking of her hips, making sure to keep pressure in the right place until she liquefied beneath them.

"Take a break," Cash said quietly as he traded spots with Aarav. "Hold her. Tell her how amazing that was. And I'll get her warmed up again for you."

"I don't think..." Sola opened one eye as she regained enough mental faculties to pick up on their discussion.

"We're not asking you to do that. Just feel." Cash stroked her inner thigh, then began kissing her, growing ever closer to her center.

"Aarav." She held her arms open for him and he went into them, their chests rubbing together as their mouths connected. If she minded the taste of her own arousal on his lips, she didn't act like it, devouring him even as Cash worked his magic.

It was probably another ten minutes of Cash's painstaking treatment, or maybe more, before she began to stiffen in his arms.

"You feel that, Aarav?" Cash asked. "Her muscles are gathering for another orgasm. Get ready. She'll be prepared for you after this."

His cock throbbed, his balls drawn tight to his body for so long they ached with the need for release.

"Yes! Yes!" Sola screamed, and came on Cash's face as if the thought of being joined with him was enough to push her over the edge.

Aarav murmured to her through the whole thing as he held her close. "You're incredible. Gorgeous. The most amazing thing I've ever seen. Damn, you're beautiful when you're coming. That's right. Give him everything you have."

She blinked up at him. "Are you sure you've never done this with anyone else? You're awfully good at it."

"Just think how much better he'll be with some practice." Cash lifted his head before placing one last, lingering kiss on Sola's thigh. "Let's be realistic, though. He's a man, not a super hero. He's not going to last very long when he gets inside you. Not this first time."

"First time?" Aarav hoped he didn't disappoint either of them.

"There'll be more," Cash promised. "We're not leaving this bedroom until every one of us has had their fill."

"Oh." Aarav wasn't about to argue. Instead, when Cash rolled to the side and patted the mattress between Sola's legs, Aarav flew to the spot. Cash took hold of Aarav's dick again and used his grip to position Aarav. He tapped Aarav's cock against Sola's mound, creating sensations that burst along his shaft and the head where it bounced off her wet clit.

Damn, he'd missed a lot skipping to the best parts on the jet. There were so many different sources of rapture he hadn't even thought to explore. Cash's fingers slipped lower and cupped Aarav's balls, rolling them in his palm until Aarav cursed.

"Sorry." Cash grinned, proving he was anything but. "Couldn't help myself. Go ahead. Get in there. Again, slowly. Feed her just a bit at a time before taking it back out."

Aarav clamped his fingers in a ring at the base of his cock hoping he didn't flood her, or worse, spill all over her, before even getting inside.

"I need you, Aarav," Sola moaned, wrapping her hands around his wrists. And that was something he could not refuse. Cash aimed the blunt head of Aarav's dick at Sola's pussy and kept them aligned as Aarav drove forward. When resistance built, he stopped then retreated. With every reentry, she coated his shaft with more of her arousal, making it easier for him to glide into her.

She was so hot, so tight, and so damn welcoming. He slammed his eyes closed and tipped his head back so the sight of her body accepting him didn't end his ride before it had begun.

"That's good. I know it feels so fucking good." Cash brought him back to reality. "Try to hold on as long as you can. It will make it better for you too when you finally fall. She's got almost all of you now. When you bottom out, sit there for a minute. Take it in, what she feels like wrapped around you, velvety and warm."

"If you don't stop talking, I'm not going to make it that long," Aarav growled.

Sola laughed and the motions vibrated up his shaft. Aarav sank into her fully, their torsos glued together. She moaned and began to writhe beneath him, grinding her clit against his muscle.

"Have to move," Aarav gritted out between his clenched teeth.

"Do it." Cash punctuated his command with one more

smack on Aarav's ass that drove him into Sola. "Aim for a smooth motion. I'm going to tip her hips up for you. Remember the spot you felt earlier? Try to rub it every time you fuck into her."

"Oh..." Sola seemed impressed when Cash grabbed her ass and lifted her, allowing Aarav to do as directed. Aarav concentrated on his task instead of the fireworks going off in his groin, but the more he landed it right, the tighter Sola got and things started to fall apart.

His strokes turned jerky and a little rough as he lost control.

"None of that." Cash jammed a pillow under Sola to free up his hands. He knelt behind Aarav and trapped his hips in his grip instead. He guided Aarav's hips in a full, fluid arc. In and out. In and out.

And when Aarav was certain he couldn't hold on a moment longer, Sola clamped down on his dick, making it nearly impossible to move at all.

"Your turn, Aarav. Fill that pussy. Show her how fucking incredible it feels when she wrings you dry like that." Cash let go.

Free to fuck at will, Aarav went wild. His hips pistoned as he tried his best to prolong Sola's rapture. Every part of his body stretched to its limit before he erupted, pouring his release deep into Sola, splattering her still-spasming flesh with his seed.

Cash gave them a moment to float, to spin through space together and cling to each other as they rode their shared orgasm to completion.

But far too soon, he was nudging Aarav aside. "Let me get in there before she cools off all the way."

Aarav withdrew, leaving a pearly trail across her entrance. Sola moaned at the loss and tugged him up the bed. But when he would have lain down and kissed her as Cash set his own cock in the bead of Aarav's come, notched at her core, Cash shook his head.

"Let her suck you while we fuck. She's going to get you ready for a proper run now that you've let off some of the pressure."

Aarav couldn't imagine improving on what they'd just done. But neither did he want to deprive Sola of the maximum enjoyment she could take from his body. So he nodded.

She opened her mouth and reached for him, drawing him into her mouth.

Aarav gasped and Cash braced him with a hand on his shoulder. He chuckled. "Give it a minute. You'll get less sensitive...and then more."

"I don't think more is possible." A bead of sweat rolled down Aarav's temple.

Sola smiled around him, suckling contentedly as Cash drew some pattern over her pussy with his cock, accustoming her to being touched again. She gave a blissful sigh when Cash entered the barest bit inside her.

Her mouth on Aarav was new and fresh and overwhelming in the best of ways. Even though he'd emptied himself inside her so completely he'd risked turning his sac inside out, the swish of her tongue and the vibrations of her purrs as Cash slid deeper within her began to stiffen Aarav's cock once more.

Now, though, there was less urgency and more intention.

Aarav watched as Cash very gradually lifted Sola from low-level arousal to something needier. He lost track of time as Sola drew on his cock and Cash treated her to a long, measured fuck that had more in common with a slow dance than what Aarav had thought sex would look like.

He realized he'd missed out on a lot, but he wanted to discover every nuance with Sola.

And maybe Cash too.

When Sola began to pant and her sucks grew unsteady, Aarav withdrew from her mouth and sat beside her instead, cradling her head in his lap. She looked up at him, her eyes glazed over, and asked, "Is it okay if I come with another man buried inside me? 'Cause I really, *really* want to do that. Right now."

Cash chuckled, though his amusement seemed strained, making Aarav aware that even he had his limits.

Aarav dusted stray wisps of hair from her face and said, "Yeah. I want to see you do that for him. For us both. I could never get tired of watching and knowing we're making you feel good. Go ahead, Sola. Fly."

She did, arching in his hold even as Cash sped up his pace, plowing into her with strokes that joined them completely before retreating so far Aarav was shocked he didn't fall out. He kept drilling into her relentlessly as Sola fisted the sheets and her honed muscles stood out in relief beneath her creamy skin. She screamed her relief.

Aarav figured he'd be heading for the bathroom soon to finish what she had started. But when she finally opened her eyes, she pouted at Cash, who was flushed and clenching his jaw, before accusing, "You didn't come with me."

Cash grinned, something fierce and wicked and so damn sexy Aarav felt a flare of attraction race through every nerve ending in his body. "Not yet. Let's go, Aarav."

11

———

Sola had known her friends were ridiculously satisfied with their relationships, especially Kennedy and Laurel, who had a pair of boyfriends each. But she was going to rip them a new one next time they hung out for not explaining to her precisely how incredible it was to be the subject of the attention of two potent, virile men.

Aarav alone was enough to give her a heart attack if she wasn't careful. But this...

Her bones had liquefied several orgasms ago, and yet there they were, side by side, staring at her like dogs eying a juicy steak they fully intended to devour.

She might not survive long enough to give her friends hell.

"How should we do this?" Aarav looked over at Cash. The time for taking turns seemed to have come to an end since both men were sporting massive erections that Sola was greedy enough to crave even after everything they'd already given her.

"Get on your back." Cash gave Aarav a gentle shove,

knocking him into place. He hadn't stopped bouncing before he reached for her and drew her over him like a blanket. She didn't even have enough functioning brain cells left to care that she was essentially boneless as she draped over his torso, lighting up every place that they came into contact.

He kissed the side of her face and whispered sweet things to her as Cash settled behind them, between both of their splayed legs. He wrapped her hair around his fist and used the hold to pull her head back, exposing her neck to Aarav. He didn't hesitate, the two men now working in tandem without having to say much.

Sola hoped Aarav realized that while she'd sleep with plenty of people, there weren't many men she'd allow to put their teeth so close to her jugular. She trusted him, had faith in him, and—yes—loved him. Cash certainly understood and played them both expertly, bringing them closer even if his own future with them was uncertain.

"You ready for the grand finale?" Cash murmured in her ear.

When she nodded—as much as she could, given his grip—he released her, instead taking hold of her hips. His wide hands spanned her waist, lifting her so that Aarav could adjust himself and when Cash settled her back down, she sheathed Aarav in a single effortless motion. Maybe there was something to his theory about taking it slow.

Sola planted her palms on Aarav's chest and followed her instincts, working him as best she could. Now it was her turn to experience Cash's palm warming her ass and she didn't mind it in the least. When his fingers slipped into her crack, she knew he meant for both of them to take her at once. Him in her ass, while Aarav filled her pussy.

And she wasn't complaining.

So it surprised her when Aarav cleared his throat. "Are you planning to do what I think you are?"

Sola wondered if that grossed him out. She should have known better.

"Yeah. Why? You want to try it? We can switch places." Cash was a generous and skilled lover.

"No. I want to do something else. Something I heard James talking about." Oh boy. Who only knew what ideas James had put in Aarav's head? He was certainly one of the advanced operators Aarav had called sexperts earlier.

"What?" she asked him, wanting to give him his dreams after he'd fulfilled so many of hers.

"Can we both... I mean, can he join me? Will it hurt you?" Aarav looked to Cash then, and Sola was certain that if the other man refused, Aarav wouldn't argue.

Cash glanced at Sola and shrugged one shoulder. "I'm game if you are. If it's uncomfortable, we'll stop and try my way."

"Son of a bitch, Aarav." Sola quaked over him, her desire instantly rekindled.

"You don't have to. It just sounded, uh, like the women enjoyed it." Aarav cursed, then came clean. "And the men too. James and Marcus were talking about how it felt with Neil and Knox's cocks rubbing theirs while they were buried in their women."

"Less talking. More action." Cash had clearly reached the end of his very, very long rope.

"I couldn't possibly be wetter or more prepared. Your forty-five minutes passed at least ten lifetimes ago." Sola figured they'd been at it for hours. It was going to take something with some edge to get her off again. And she found that although she'd already come more times than she could count, she desperately wanted the three of them to reach this final peak together, no matter how unlikely that was.

"You promise to tell us if it hurts?" Aarav held her still until she nodded.

"How the hell did I get this lucky?" Cash muttered as if to himself. "The two of you are hot as fuck and you're letting me be part of this?"

He laid his palm between her shoulder blades and pressed until her chest was mashed to Aarav's, doing nothing to lessen her anticipation. They made out, and while they did, Cash's cock probed at the place where they were joined.

Aarav hissed as Cash's dick slid along his and stretched Sola around them. She was relaxed, incredibly prepared, and so damn glad when holding the two of them inside her widened her eyes, and her pussy.

"Holy fuck." She crushed her mouth to Aarav's and kissed him furiously as he and Cash developed some sort of unspoken plan that involved Aarav burying himself in her as Cash withdrew and then Aarav pulling back so Cash could advance, all the while slipping across each other as she held them bundled together.

Sola lost track of who was touching her where. Someone massaged her breasts while someone else kissed her and they both fucked the shit out of her. All she could do was cling to them and hold on as a storm of passion raged around her. Aarav's earlier orgasm and Cash's monumental restraint meant they didn't race for the finish either.

They worked her, and each other inside her, endlessly

as her body adjusted to holding them both then began to climb inexorably toward climax.

"Shit." Cash growled and bit her shoulder. "This is a first for me too, but it won't be a last. I can feel you both. You're killing me."

After so many months doubting Aarav's attraction to her, this was balm for Sola's soul in addition to pleasure for her body. There was no doubt, as she was stretched wide and held between them, that both of these men wanted her.

That deep-seated knowledge tripped something inside her, pushing her past the point of no return. "Aarav! Cash! I'm going to…"

She didn't finish her sentence because Cash roared, giving each of them the permission they needed to surrender together. "Me too. Aarav, let's go."

Aarav shuddered beneath her, lurching up as his body spasmed. Cash mimicked him, curling over her back as he embedded himself completely within her. Both men groaned and grunted as she drained them dry, making a mess of each other even as they saturated her pussy with their releases.

Sola had never experienced such blinding ecstasy as she did in those seemingly endless moments where white hot pleasure flooded every cell of her being.

Then she wasn't the only one with noodles for limbs.

The three of them collapsed into a pile in the middle of Aarav's thankfully oversized bed. Sola ended up sandwiched by them, which she did not intend to bitch about. Aarav gathered her to him, her back plastered to his front. He wrapped his top arm and leg over her, keeping her secure and warm in his hold. Cash rolled to his side so he could study them as their heartrates returned to somewhat normal even if it took longer than when she ran ten miles.

None of them spoke. She figured that was for the best because she was terrified of ruining the perfection of the moment. Especially since she was certain that she didn't only want this to be a one-night stand. And if she felt that longing for something more permanent, then Aarav certainly would.

It was likely he was already attached to Cash, if not through the same deep emotions he'd told her he had for her—thrilling her after months of anticipation and doubt —then via some intense but maybe short-lived bond created by their situation, the high stakes, and Sola's reaction to this man who'd turned her from conflicted to brazen.

But what if her attraction to Cash and where it had led them meant that Aarav got hurt?

Would it wreck the budding relationship they'd struggled so tirelessly to forge?

What they'd done, and being honest about her desires, was a huge gamble. Like Cash's dad, she might very well have gotten herself in too far. And now it was too late to go back.

She knew what this felt like. Had experienced the joy brought to her by two men who put her pleasure first and one who already held her heart. She feared she'd taken the biggest risk of her life, and she hoped it paid off.

12

Aarav cracked up as he watched Legend playing unnecessarily aggressive air hockey with his partner, Tavish. When the puck launched over the table and smacked Tavish in his iron six-pack, he unleashed a string of curses. His Scottish accent got thicker when he was agitated.

Funny, over the past two weeks Sola and Cash had said the same thing happened to Aarav when they were making love. Which they had done often in their near nightly marathon sessions. He was short on sleep but wasn't complaining one bit.

While Jordan had been consulting with experts on how to best approach the Jay Barber situation, they'd been spending every moment together, learning to live with each other and finding out how similar they were despite the different corners of the world and stations in life they'd been raised in. Even when hanging out with the larger Shields team and their families as they were now in the lounge. No one was out on assignment so they were scattered mostly between the gym, the kitchen, and this recreational area except for Laurel, Nolan, and Jace, who had snuck off to their own apartment for some afternoon alone time. They were making the most of the days before Jace left on tour with Kason later that month.

Aarav didn't blame them. Now that he'd had Sola and Cash in his bed every night, he didn't want to think about how cold and lonely it would be without them by his side.

"It's nice to see you smiling so damn much lately," James said as he plopped onto the oversized beanbag chair next to the couch the three of them were monopolizing.

"Is that your way of reminding me that you were right all along when you kept encouraging me to confess my feelings to Sola?" Aarav wondered.

"I'm subtle like that. Yup." James laced his fingers, then turned them inside out until they cracked. "Now that you're on the right track, I think I'll turn my attention to Ruby, Ace, and Liam."

Aarav, Sola, and Cash redirected their gazes to where Ruby flailed at thin air, a white virtual reality headset covering her eyes and headphones in her ears. Utterly oblivious, she had no idea that Ace and Liam were ogling her as if she were practicing on the stripper pole again instead of stumbling around looking ludicrous to anyone outside of her binary world. They clearly thought everything she did was adorable in its prime geekiness.

"They're hopeless." Aarav felt smug enough to call it like he saw it now that he wasn't the one making a fool of himself.

Sola was more serious, though. "Why do you think they haven't made a move yet? I keep telling her, like they told me, that the guys are interested, but she doesn't believe me. And I don't blame her."

James tapped his fingers on his pursed lips. "Not sure, but I think there's something between them that might be tripping them up. I'm on the case, though, don't you worry."

Aarav laughed. James on a matchmaking mission was far more terrifying than the rest of the Shields on a covert operation.

Across the seating area from them, Blakely looked up from the pictures she was taking of Knox's back and his now-healed masterpiece. She was using it as a cornerstone of her portfolio for her tattoo studio, which was opening as soon as the building was finished. It was a massive project, though, and was taking longer than expected due to the town pushing back on some of her permits. Their interference had delayed construction for months, irritating both her and Mike, the head of the Powertools crew, who was the foreman on the job.

James had often declared he was never so glad he'd decided to change careers and work with Shields instead of dealing with that legal nightmare once the Powertools had shifted their focus from manual labor to becoming foremen of individual crews.

Ace ambled over to Blakely, gesturing to his cast. "Once this is off, how long do you think I'm going to have to wait for the scars to heal where they put the pins in before I can cover them up with ink?"

"It could be a while." She winced. "Let's see what it looks like when the plaster is gone."

Ace grumbled. He hated the cast, and Aarav suspected he'd despise the reminder of his injury just as much. The Shields took it personally when they perceived they'd failed, and Ace still hadn't quite gotten over being in the wrong place at the wrong time that day or how his recovery had sidelined him from working with Liam in the field these past months.

Aarav could see why they might have some shit to work through before taking things to the next step with Ruby. But maybe he'd pull a James and offer them his perspective sometime when there weren't quite so many eyes and ears around.

James sighed when he spotted the next two people to come through the lounge doors. His wife, Devon, and husband, Neil, who grinned at James. "We're done upstairs if you're ready to go home. It'll be nice to have an early night for once. Maybe we can swing by Devra's and pick up some take out to eat in bed, huh?"

James had an apartment on site for all-night ops, but his primary residence was in the cluster of homes the Powertools had constructed along the lake behind the Hot Rods garage. Joe and Eli were cousins and their extended families sprawled through the wooded area. Close yet with their own personal space too.

"That sounds like heaven." James held his arms up and Neil bent to lift him out of the bean sac. James put his legs around Neil's waist and kissed his husband before sliding down his front, then spinning to treat Devon to an equally enthusiastic greeting.

"So did they finally make their mind up?" James pointed over their head to where Kennedy and Marcus's apartments were being combined. They had the other two units on the same floor as Aarav and Sola, and Aarav would have been lying if he said he wasn't wondering what their similar options might be down the road if things worked out as he hoped they would.

"For the moment." Devon shrugged. "Don't bitch,

baby. You all just continue requesting renovations and keep Powertools in business. Job security."

Blakely shook her head at that. "Between my shop, this place, the work on Bare Natural 2 for Kayla, your own damn houses, and who knows what else, I think you have more work than you could handle with a hundred crews."

"She's right." James sulked. "It's going to take twenty years to work through it all and I hate it when you work late."

"So say your goodbyes and let's take advantage right now." Neil took James's hand in his and squeezed. "You can ride with us and leave your death-trap pea on wheels here. I'll drop you off on my way in tomorrow since I'll be spending another month or so on the site upstairs."

James crossed his arms and huffed. "I'll have you know it's been reinforced. Not even a head-on collision could do anything to it."

"Let's not test that theory." Neil winced. Their close friend, and sometimes lover, Dave had suffered a near fatal accident. Though it had been over a decade ago, some memories never faded enough.

Mark—a teenager James had taken under his wing, who was now Devon's protégé at Powertools—trotted in as he caught up with them. He stared at James with abject admiration. "This place is so cool. Can I stay and hang out with you?"

"You're always welcome at Shields, same as Powertools." James fist-bumped him. "But I'm actually leaving. I need to find my keys and then I'm heading out."

Neil shook his head at James's stubbornness. When James patted his pocket, a rumble that certainly should not have come from a tiny car like his reverberated off the plate glass of the lounge, which faced the side parking lot.

James had refused to park in the back since the tree had crushed his car's roof in a freak summer storm.

"What's that?" Mark asked.

"Oh no! I think I hit the remote start button." James fished the fob from his tight jeans and smashed it a thousand times in a row, trying to get it to turn off again.

"What's the big deal?" Aarav asked around a chuckle.

"It's moving! I must have forgotten to set the parking brake this morning." James howled as he dashed to the window. All their friends ran behind him in time to watch the absurd auto trundle across the inclined lot, picking up enough speed to hop the curb at the end of it and plunge down the embankment into the retention pond at the bottom of the hill with an impressive splash.

The aeration fountain at the center sprayed cheerily over the vehicle as it began to sink, giant bubbles disturbing the family of ducks swimming past. They hopped up onto the hood and promptly took a nervous poop on James's fresh paint job.

James plopped onto his ass on the floor, his legs crossed as he wailed in disbelief. Everyone else in the room, however, roared with laughter. Aarav doubled over, Sola shaking against his side, until moisture gathered at the corner of his eyes.

"What the hell is wrong with you all?" Cash asked as he stared in disbelief.

"We'll explain later. When I can breathe." Sola clutched her ribs.

Their chaos was enough to draw Ruby's attention. She blinked as she rejoined them in the real world. And when she saw James's car had become the latest addition to the landscape, she too lost it.

Neil drew out his phone and hit a favorite contact.

"Bryce, you're never going to guess what just happened. Can you bring the flatbed? Don't forget the winch, you're going to need it."

They were still rolling with laughter when Jordan came into the room, looking anything but amused. He waved his finger at Cash, Aarav, and Sola. "You three. Come with me. Ruby, you too."

And like that, the fun times were over.

13

Cash swallowed hard as he looked from Aarav to Sola, who were flanking him where they sat across from Jordan in the command center. Ruby jogged in behind them and took her station at the brains of the room.

Jordan didn't bother with civilities. That wasn't the kind of meeting this was going to be. He could already tell from the lines around the boss man's eyes and the ones creasing his forehead. Cash didn't envy the impossible weight of the responsibility he bore.

"Okay, so you know we've been working on how to hamstring these gunrunning bastards by cutting off their funding, which is really only half the battle until we can go after them more directly." Jordan looked at Cash while he spoke, but Aarav and Sola were nodding along.

"Yeah." It still seemed surreal how close he'd come to not being there, especially since he had fuck all to do with his father's gambling operations.

"Well, I've worked a few miracles, and was able to negotiate a deal for your father. It would grant him full immunity, which I'm sure he does not deserve and took an awful lot of convincing to arrange." Jordan rubbed his eyes. When was the last time he'd slept?

"Damn, that's great news." Sola clasped Cash's hand, but he didn't quite share her enthusiasm.

"Why are you telling me this?" Cash wondered.

"Because I need you to convince him to take it." Jordan grimaced.

"Of course I'll try, but..." Cash thought despite what he'd shared with them, they still didn't fully understand how little his father respected him and vice versa. However, some dumb part of him still wished it were different. Maybe this could be the turning point for their relationship.

"I have a plan, just play along." Jordan pointed to Aarav and Sola. "You two, look grumpy, like you used to before Cash showed up."

He hoped that was true. Smiling a tiny bit, he gave in. "Yeah. Okay. Let's do it."

"Ruby, can you put us through to Mr. Kalykalaos on videochat using the private line Cash gave us from his contacts?" Jordan asked.

"On it." She tapped a few screens. Before Cash had a chance to really get himself ready, the device was ringing.

The first test would be to see if his father even bothered to answer. He might only because he didn't recognize the number as Cash's. That thought stung.

It took seven rings, but just as Cash was giving up hope, his father appeared on the huge curved screen of the command center, making him look entirely too real and too close.

"I knew I shouldn't have picked that up." Cash's father

glowered at his son. He felt the impact of that disdain even from half the world away.

"Wait. Mr. Kalykalaos. Don't hang up." Jordan's words were an order, not a request. "Not if you want to see your son alive again."

Well, shit. Was that the plan? Cash could have told Jordan his dad didn't give a fuck and would probably pay the gunrunners a bonus if they offed Cash so long as it didn't blow back on him.

Looking bored, his father seemed like he was going to disconnect anyway, sending a knife through Cash's heart. Not that he hadn't expected as much, but it still rankled to know his father probably hadn't even noticed he was gone. Hell, Sola and Aarav and even Mr. Prickles probably gave more of a damn and they'd only known him for a few weeks.

"Really? You're wasting my time with this bullshit?" His father was irritated but also obviously curious or he would already have bailed. "Whoever you are, fucking up my grand opening, acting like barbarians and scaring off my customers, making my *associates* none too happy with the missed opportunities that would have come with those high stakes games...you can go fuck yourself. And take him with you. He's only ever been a pain in my ass and a disgrace to our family."

"So you were hoping we'd eliminate him instead of you. Is that why you were using him as a shield?" Jordan asked, one brow raised.

"I sure as shit didn't want to be standing out on an exposed balcony knowing my *partners* have plenty of enemies. No thanks. Looks like I was right, too."

Aarav clenched his jaw so hard Cash swore he heard the man's poor teeth grind together, and Sola gripped the arms of her chair as tightly as she had clutched him while dangling over the ocean that fateful day. The day they'd saved him, when he hadn't even known he'd needed it.

Cash would likely have gone off right then and said fuck it to the whole thing, but Jordan shot him a silent plea. He only conceded because he was aware that what was going down was bigger than only his fucked-up relationship with his father. This could change many lives.

He thought of the photographs he'd seen when he'd researched the marketplace massacre and other atrocities linked to the gunrunners his father had helped fund.

Jordan cleared his throat. "I see you're a logical man. So I have an offer for you. I can grant you immunity. You won't have to watch your back anymore, creating decoys to protect yourself. I've talked to the relevant agencies and the US government is willing to shelter you if you cease operations and provide information that leads to the demise of your *collaborators*, as you've called them."

Cash's father cackled at that. "Let me guess. You're going to take my money, put me up in a series of shitty motels where I'll have to give up everything I enjoy about life and live like a peon until they track me down and end me for being disloyal? Get the fuck out."

Cash could have told Jordan his father would never agree to those terms. That didn't mean Cash wasn't disappointed anyway.

Jordan tried again. "Mr. Kalykalaos, this might not be what you envisioned for your future, but at least you'd have one. If you reject our assistance, I guarantee you're signing your own death warrant. Because there isn't a way forward that doesn't end up with you caught in the crossfire. Either you'll be taken out by enemies of your friends, or they'll take care of you themselves when you're no longer useful to them. And I promise you, that day is coming. We will shut you down one way or another. Them too."

"Are you trying to scare me?" Cash's father snorted dismissively. "You're like a kid wearing a vaguely creepy mask on Halloween compared to them. If they wanted to send me a message, they wouldn't have a corporate videoconference about it. They'd cut my fucking dick off and feed it to me to make a point. I realize now that I got more than I bargained for when I took their help. But I'm going to make the most of it while I can. I'd rather go out on top than cower in the dirt—like my pathetic son—until my time is up."

"Cash isn't your concern anymore." Jordan would only take so much and it appeared that was the line. "We've got him and we'll be looking out for him like his mother would have insisted on. That's why you slowly, painfully poisoned her to make it look as if she was ill, isn't it? Because she took his side and not yours? She tried to keep you from emotionally abusing him and threatened to leave with him, but you couldn't have that messing with your reputation now, could you?"

Grief and horror strangled Cash. He sat up perfectly straight, gasping for air, and absorbed every nuance of his father's expression as Jordan flung accusations that every person in the room could tell were true. He hadn't known the details, but his gut had always suspected even if he didn't want to believe it. But now, it made so much sense.

Under the table, Sola took his hand and Aarav clasped his thigh, just over his knee. They lent him their strength and promised silently that he wasn't alone.

"Do you think I'm about to incriminate myself? I'm not that stupid. Keep your useless 'help' and fuck these games you're playing. My wife was soft and weak, exactly like the child she burdened me with."

Jordan looked to Cash then. "We tried. If you have anything to say to this sack of shit, I recommend you do it now."

Cash considered for a moment, then uttered a single word, knowing it was final. "Goodbye."

His father gave him the finger, then cut their connection, leaving Cash staring at an empty black screen.

14

S ola sat at the kitchen table with Aarav as Cash paced back and forth. "Why don't you come sit down? We can go hang out in the living room if you want? Watch the rest of that murder mystery series you started the other night?"

"Doesn't sound very entertaining when it's too much like real life." Cash rubbed a hand over his hair. "I need to do something. Aarav, you want some tea?"

When did he not? He was addicted to the stuff.

"Uh, yeah. That sounds good. But I can make it..." Aarav squirmed in his chair and though he was trying to be polite, Sola knew what he wasn't saying. He was extremely particular about it and there's no way someone could get the ten thousand intricate steps correct to make it exactly as he liked.

"I've got it." Cash pulled out the canister of loose leaf tea and Aarav's favorite mug, set the kettle to what looked about right to Sola, then arranged the spoon rest, sugar, and milk exactly as Aarav did while he waited for the water to come up to temperature. He preset the shiny silver steeping timer for four minutes and thirty-seven seconds.

"Wow. You've really been paying attention." Aarav finger-combed his beard.

"It's important to you." Cash shrugged one shoulder. The tea ritual seemed to settle him some as he focused on getting each precise detail correct and doing something for someone he—Sola suspected—cared for.

Thing was, as often as they'd slept together in the past several weeks, the men had always made her the focus. As decadent as it was, being so greedy, it worried her. Where did they stand with each other? They were friends, certainly, but hadn't really crossed the line into lovers, not in the sense that she'd consider them to be dating if she weren't also in the picture. Was that how these sorts of relationships worked? Or was that a chink in their armor?

She hadn't pushed the issue because, frankly, she was being selfish, having too much fun being shared by them to risk it falling apart by asking difficult questions. And also because she was hoping that in time, as Aarav developed an emotional connection to Cash, things between them would evolve.

After all, it had taken him the best part of a year to embrace his attraction to her even when their career and living situation had forced them into intense bonding situations. This could be a start, though, if they could help Cash work through the obvious wounds his father had ripped wide open earlier.

Sola rose and crossed to him, hugging him from behind as he concentrated on preparing Aarav's brew. "I'm sorry your dad is an asshole."

If that wasn't a greeting card yet, she thought it should be.

"That's not news, is it?" Cash sagged in her hold. "What's fucking with my head more is finding out I was responsible for my mother's death."

"Where the hell did you get an idea like that?" Aarav stood too, clutching Cash's shoulder and turning him around until he faced them both. "I heard Jordan say your *father* was at fault. Not you."

"He attacked her because of me." He stared at the floor, unwilling to look them in the eye.

"It sounds to me like your mom was a decent human being. I'm sure if it hadn't been that particular reason, assuming he's even telling the truth, then it would have been something else. He doesn't seem like he takes kindly to people questioning his decisions or beliefs."

"You could be right." When the kettle beeped, Cash turned around and poured the steamy water over the tea leaves until they were fully submerged and initiated the steeping timer before facing them again.

"Tell me if I'm wrong, but I think part of the problem is that you hate that you still give a shit about him." Aarav surprised Sola by leaning in and hugging Cash, who reciprocated the embrace. Unwilling to be left out, Sola ducked under their elbows and put an arm around each of her lovers. "It's okay to love him, you know? None of our parents were perfect. That doesn't change how we saw them as children or how badly we wish we could have changed them."

Sola peered over at Aarav. He didn't often open up like this and certainly not with just anyone. Her heart skipped as she realized he was forming the emotional connection he needed to take things to the next level with Cash, whether he admitted it to himself or not.

She grabbed each of them by their shirts and tugged

them into the bedroom, where they could be near and cozy and safe as they laid bare these traumatic wounds.

"Aarav never talks about his childhood. If it wasn't for his accent, I wouldn't even know he was from India," Sola said as she scooted backward onto the bed and drew her men to her. They sat in a triangle with their legs crisscrossed, their knees touching.

Aarav looked down at the beat-up watch on his wrist and sighed. He rubbed the gouged face with the pad of his thumb, then looked at them both. "We were poor, though I didn't realize it then. Me, my seven brothers and sisters, our parents, and our three surviving grandparents lived in a two-bedroom apartment in a building stuck into the side of a hill. It was a big step up from the slums my parents had grown up in, and my father worked incredibly hard to keep us there."

Sola took one of his hands and Cash the other. Then they clasped their free hands until all three of them were joined and healing energy flowed between them.

"It didn't start on purpose, but my friend Suresh and I liked to perform. We would sing our own made-up songs and dance along. One day a crowd started gathering around us and people threw us some coins. We were so excited, so we did it again and again, and soon we had enough to buy a used radio. After maybe a month, we had enough that we took it to our families."

Sola couldn't believe she'd never seen him dance before. Why hadn't he joined her at Sevan's reception? Next time she would pull him onto the floor for sure.

"Suresh's family was thrilled. They bought food and told him to skip school to perform more." Aarav's fingers trembled in hers. "My father, though, was horrified. He said he wasn't doing all he was to lift us up for me to go out and act like a street rat. He refused the money and forbade me from hanging out with Suresh."

"I'm sorry, Aarav." Sola imagined what it would have done to him to be told he couldn't help. She'd bet even as a child he'd been noble to the core. "If nothing else, that you had to stop doing something you enjoyed so much with your friend."

He looked up at her then. "I didn't."

"Oh." Cash rubbed his thumb over Aarav's knuckles.

"I stayed in school, but snuck out in the evenings and joined Suresh." His eyes focused far in the distance as if staring back into time when he said, "And that's why I wasn't home when the earthquake hit. Our building was shoddy, overcrowded, and falling down even when the ground wasn't shaking."

"You don't have to tell us the rest." Cash winced.

"I still wonder to this day if I had been there, if I could have made a difference. If I could have dug out and saved them. My father's arm was sticking up from rubble. I recognized it from his watch. This watch. He almost made it out. I was the oldest and the strongest of my siblings. If I was there..."

"You probably would have died, too." Sola felt a shiver run down her spine at the thought. She suddenly understood his need to protect others, even if they never knew of the sacrifices he made for them.

"You were right, Aarav. None of our parents were perfect. Your dad should have encouraged your passion, and Cash's father should have supported him, and mine... well, I wish how much I loved my mom had been enough to overcome her grief. But it wasn't. And none of that is on us. All we can do is try to learn from their mistakes and be better. It's okay to survive. It's okay to be happy. And I bet that if we could talk to any of our moms right now, that's what they'd want for us."

"But do we deserve it? Do *I*?" Aarav wondered. "If my dad despised me dancing on the street, I'm pretty sure he'd be horrified that I kill people for a very lucrative living."

"Have you been carrying that around this whole time?" Sola narrowed her eyes at him. "What you do is save people from the dregs of humanity. You know that, right?"

"In theory. But I can relate to Cash, I guess." Aarav looked directly into his eyes, and when their gazes locked on one another, Sola thought she saw something there that hadn't existed before. Recognition. A spark. Emotions that went deeper than a mutual desire for her.

"Because you've never felt worthy of being loved? And so you couldn't imagine that anyone else might believe differently?" Cash supplied.

Aarav nodded.

Nothing could keep Sola from them then. She launched herself in their direction, bowling both of them over so they ended up lying side by side with her splayed over them.

"I'm here to prove you both wrong." Sola kissed each of them in turn before going back for seconds.

"If we'd never met Cash, I don't think I would have been able to see from an outside perspective how fucked up I've been." Aarav combed his fingers through Cash's hair.

Cash burst out laughing at that. "I'm happy my issues were good for something."

"Without that understanding... Without realizing everyone is deserving of the love someone else is willing to give us, maybe Sola and I never would have lasted. Now at least we have a shot." Aarav leaned toward Cash and murmured, "I owe you more than you realize."

Then Sola sat back so she could watch as the men kissed for the first time. They were gentle yet determined and both so confident she felt certain they'd needed to find each other as much as she'd needed them both in her life and her bed.

After plenty of soft sighs escalated to groans between each other's parted lips, their beards rasping together, Cash angled himself for a deeper taste. He probed Aarav's smile with his tongue until Aarav let him in and began to suck on it.

Sola didn't even try to hide how much seeing them together, pleasing each other, turned her on. She shucked her shirt and leggings so she could touch herself as she observed them making out. They'd spent weeks spoiling her. Now it was her turn to witness them take from each other.

Cash wasn't stopping with a simple kiss either. His hand disappeared under Aarav's long-sleeved cream shirt before undoing the three buttons at the top with his teeth so that he could nuzzle the base of Aarav's throat. He stroked Aarav's abs and up to his chest while his hips began to rock, rubbing his stiffening cock on Aarav's thigh.

"Damn, you two are sexy." Sola made sure they knew how much she admired the view. She allowed her moan to ring out when she slipped one finger between her legs to rub her clit.

Both men whipped their heavy gazes to her. As if by tacit understanding, Cash rolled off Aarav long enough for them to make their clothes vanish. And shortly, they were stretched out in front of her, all bronze skin and dark hair and hard cocks.

Instead of pouncing on her like they had every chance they'd gotten the past several weeks, they eyed each other. Cash smirked at Aarav. "I think your girlfriend likes this."

Aarav chuckled at that, and she was glad he didn't deny that they were more to each other than co-workers or fuck buddies. It was progress, although they'd never formally laid out exactly what their relationship status was. "Well then, why don't we put on a show for her? Let her see what she can look forward to."

Cash didn't fuck around. He reached between Aarav's legs and fisted his cock. Aarav took his cue and mirrored the other man, his fingers encircling the base of Cash's erection. They examined each other, getting used to the similar yet different sensation of touching someone else's body as intimately as their own.

Their cocks reflected their general stature. Aarav's was thicker than Cash's, but Cash was longer, same as he was taller. Both got the job done just fine. They sat facing each other, their legs knitted as they jerked each other off while leaning toward each other to continue refining the way their mouths came together. As they settled in, they grew bolder and less tentative, their exchange reminding Sola of the sparring matches she'd witnessed in the Shields' gym. They tested each other, pushed the boundaries, and kept going when they realized they could handle the intense reaction they were inspiring in each other.

It was fascinating and beautiful to watch them discover this new facet of their relationship, and how they fit together as more than her accessories. Sola leaned back on the pillows and spread her legs wider, her hands wandering over her stomach and breasts, then back to her pussy.

And when a spurt of Aarav's precome slicked Cash's hand, she moaned, drawing their attention.

Aarav blinked, dazed, before glancing at her then down at Cash's cock, which was fully aroused and flushed in Aarav's grip. He licked his lips and Cash groaned.

"You want to blow him, don't you?" Sola asked.

Aarav swallowed hard, then met Cash's blazing gaze with a curt nod. "I've never done that before. I might suck at it."

"That's sort of the point." Cash was as encouraging with Aarav's passion as he'd been with hers. He accepted everything they gave him and soaked it up as if he'd been in an affection drought for most of his life, which she suspected was the truth. Although he had more physical experience than Aarav, she had a feeling this emotional bond was completely new, and slightly terrifying for him. "You can try anything you want with me. Go ahead."

Cash lay back, propping himself up on his elbows so he didn't miss a moment of Aarav shifting forward. Rather than open his mouth and slurp Cash's cock to the base in a rush, he took it slow, appreciating every inch of Cash from his neck to his collarbones, across his lightly furred chest and down his flat stomach. The whole time, Aarav's hands glided over Cash's ripped arms and whatever else he could reach.

And when his lips finally grazed along the underside of Cash's cock, which rested long and heavy on his belly, Cash cursed. But he still didn't hurry Aarav, instead submitting to the unintentional torture as he learned his way around another man's body.

Sola's pussy clenched as Aarav extended his tongue

and swiped from the base of Cash's cock all the way to the tip, pausing to lap at the pearly fluid at the tip. Cash's head fell back momentarily and he clutched the sheets as if to keep from framing Aarav's head and using the grip to fuck his face.

"Damn, that feels good." Cash's voice was rougher now, strained as he held back and let Aarav play with him.

Sola couldn't stop staring as Aarav lifted Cash's cock and put it in his mouth for the first time, his throat flexing as he swallowed and sucked and fed himself inch after inch. Cash collapsed backward on the bed, silently begging the ceiling for the strength to hold out so Aarav could take his fill.

He surprised her when he flung his arm out and shackled her ankle, and even more when he yanked her toward him. "Aarav shouldn't get to have all the fun. Come here and sit on my face."

Sola put her hand on his shoulder to brace herself. "Wait, not like that. I want to see."

She turned around so she was straddling Cash's head but facing Aarav, who now bobbed slowly and steadily over Cash's length.

Cash wrapped his arm around her waist, then pinned her to him, his mouth and nose first nuzzling her to accustom her to the vibrant sensations, only amplified by the vision Aarav made as he devoured Cash.

Cash laid the base of his palm on her mound and used his fingers to rub circles on her clit while his tongue mimicked the pace of Aarav's mouth over his cock on her pussy. She had no idea how he was holding out, if what Aarav was doing to Cash felt half as good as what Cash was doing to her.

She clearly had the hair-trigger between the three of

them. But how could she resist temptation when they were so damn fine and knew exactly how to please her?

Sola cupped her breasts, pinching her nipples as her hips grew restless, rocking her pussy over Cash's mouth. Aarav looked up at her and met her gaze with Cash's dick embedded in his mouth, so deep now it must have been in his throat.

A spasm wrung her pussy, slicking Cash's face.

Aarav pulled off Cash only long enough to say, "You're going to make her come, Cash. You're so good at that."

Cash grunted in response, double when Aarav sank over him once more, slipping his hand between Cash's thighs to handle his balls. Cash planted his feet on the mattress and his hips fucked upward in sync with the thrusting of his tongue into her pussy.

And this time when Aarav looked back at her, watching another man feast on her while he went down on the guy, she couldn't hold back.

Without warning, an orgasm washed over her, making her cry out. Cash pinned her and kept her steady as her entire body clenched and released. Aarav rose then, carefully straddling Cash so he could kiss her while she showed both men just how much she loved seeing them together. He tasted of musk and man and carnal possibilities.

Aarav ran his hands over her arms and back, cuddling her to his chest when her muscles relaxed entirely. After a while, with her head on his shoulder as she recovered, she realized he was essentially sitting on Cash, who was massaging her ass and telling her how much he loved seeing her unravel.

When she shifted, Aarav did too, then went stiff all over. Cash groaned.

"Sorry," Aarav said breathily as he set Sola gently aside, where she melted into the mattress beside them. Which was when she realized what had happened.

Aarav had backed up on Cash's dick, which had prodded him in the ass. And now they were hovering there, staring at each other as if wondering who was going to be first to admit where they hoped this would go.

"Is that what you want?" Sola asked them both, since neither of them seemed to be able to unfreeze themselves long enough to take that next step.

Aarav cleared his throat, then looked at her. "Would you mind?"

"Do you really think I would?" She leaned in and kissed him so thoroughly he could have no doubt about how desperately she wanted him to be as happy as he'd made her.

Aarav nodded slightly. "Then yes. I want. Fuck me, Cash?"

Sola was shocked when Cash didn't pounce on Aarav immediately. What the hell?

Then she saw the doubt lingering in his eyes despite what Aarav had shared with him. She brushed the hair from his face and kissed his brow before murmuring in his ear, "You're worthy of this and everything good that comes your way. You deserve to be happy."

Cash squeezed his eyes closed and nodded.

"You do too." Sola sat up and kissed Aarav again.

"Then I need you both to help me do something I've been dying to try for a while."

"What?" Cash asked, seemingly incapable of uttering more than that single word with the anticipation of what they were about to do buzzing through the air.

"I want you to fuck me while I fuck Sola."

15

Aarav couldn't believe he'd uttered his fantasy out loud when he'd kept the desire confined to his daydreams before then. Until he'd had a deeper connection with Cash, it had only been a passing thought, a curiosity, but now that something had shifted between them, he needed it to be real. To know what it felt like to be held between the two people he had fallen for.

There was no denying it—not to himself, and not to them—when his body reacted like this to them both. It had been terrifying to acknowledge the depth of his attachment when it had happened with Sola, had taken him months to accept it and longer to act on it. So doing the same with not only her but also Cash, so soon, could have stalled him out.

Luckily, Sola was there.

"I'd like that too. I can promise you, having done that myself, that it's going to be incredible." She reached up and laced their fingers together, using the hold to pull him on top of her. Her presence alone reminded him of the consequences of making the same mistakes again. He'd almost missed out on being intimate with her and he'd hurt her while he struggled with his demons. So he trusted that she was right and had faith that if he was honest and open, everything would work out.

Cash and Sola rewarded him by making his steamiest imaginings come true.

Cash rose to his knees. He hooked one hand behind Aarav's neck and the other behind Sola's, alternating crushing his mouth to each of theirs and showing them exactly how excited he was at the prospect of taking their relationship to a new level.

"How do you want me?" Aarav rasped, eager now that he'd come clean about what he craved.

"Patient." Cash's smile spread slowly, making Aarav realize he might have underestimated their lover. "We're not going to speed through this. I'm going to make it good for you. For us all. So you have to give me some time to get you ready first. Let's see how much stamina you've built up these past few weeks, huh?"

Aarav nodded. He appreciated they were looking out for him when his libido had gone from dormant to hyperactive and dragged his unprepared body along with it.

"So first, I want you to get inside Sola. She's going to hold you for me while I work. Get good and riled up so you can accept me easily." Cash stroked down Aarav's back from his shoulder to the curve of his ass, squeezing his cheeks and pulling them the barest bit apart before spanking him hard. "Go on. Fuck her. Slowly. You're going to need to last a while."

Aarav was used to taking orders. He encircled the base of his cock and aimed it toward Sola, who spread her legs and gave him plenty of room to maneuver. He ran the tip up and down her drenched folds to lubricate it before using two fingers on top of his shaft to angle his dick just right before he advanced.

She sighed as he slid home and sank within her tight heat.

"Very nice," Cash cooed as he watched from behind while Aarav's hard-on disappeared into their woman. It seemed normal and casual when Cash reached out to cup Aarav's balls—running his thumb down the center seam of the sac—and used the grip to guide Aarav, setting the unrelenting, deliberate, and painfully sluggish pace for their lovemaking. "Keep going. Bring her up again. I want us to enjoy this together."

Sola moaned. "No worries there." Her pussy hugged Aarav, rippling around him as he moved in and out of her.

"Concentrate, Aarav." Cash gripped his ass again and spread him, wider this time. "Don't you dare stop. Give her what she needs and I'll take care of you."

It seemed like an easy enough, and certainly enjoyable, task. Until Cash sank lower and buried his face in Aarav's ass, his tongue rimming Aarav's hole.

"Holy shit!" He jerked hard enough that his cock slipped from Sola's grasp and his breath lodged in his chest. The contact had been electric and so damn overwhelming in the best of ways.

"What did I tell you?" Cash slapped the other side of Aarav's flank, which did nothing to reduce his excitement. "Put it back in and I'll give you more."

Sola chuckled when Aarav fished for his cock and buried it inside her in record time.

"Sorry." He dropped his forehead to hers. "I'll try to be gentle."

"I'm not that delicate." Sola framed his face, her fingers sliding into his hair. She rubbed his scalp, distracting him a bit as Cash made contact again, this time with a long, gentle lap of his tongue that made Aarav shudder and his cock jerk inside Sola.

She did some of the work for him, rocking upward as he held perfectly still, afraid to overreact again and ruin her fun or cause Cash to stop whatever the hell he was doing back there to make it feel so fucking great.

When Sola directed his head toward hers, it was automatic to kiss her, enjoying the softness of her lips and the steel of her muscles against his. They might be covered in soft, pale skin, but she was as strong underneath as he was. Hell, far more.

She dragged her fingers down his back, scratching lightly. "You're so sexy, Aarav. This feels incredible already."

"It does," he agreed.

And when Cash lifted his head for a moment, Aarav drew a deep shaking breath.

"Where's your lube, Aarav?" Cash replaced his tongue with the tip of one finger, pressing and teasing but not trying to penetrate. Not without ensuring his comfort first.

"Shit. I don't have any." He looked over his shoulder, horrified. "You're not going to stop, are you?"

"I'm sure as hell not going to fuck you dry. I'd never hurt you like that." Cash frowned.

Sola shifted restlessly beneath Aarav. He was glad he wasn't the only needy one. "I'm positive Marcus, Kennedy, and Knox have a gallon or two. Want me to go next door and borrow some?"

Aarav's cock lost some of its stiffness. None of the Shields would judge him, especially not when they enjoyed such similar passions, but he wasn't quite ready to share his newfound pleasures with the rest of the world. "No, don't. It's not like asking for a cup of fucking sugar from your neighbor."

"Hang on. No one's leaving this bed until I'm done with them." Cash bit Aarav's ass, returning the blood flow to his cock to max. "Sola, you use coconut oil on your hair, don't you?"

"Yes!" Her eyes widened. "There's a giant bottle in the shower."

"That'll work." Cash smacked Aarav's ass again and said, "Did I tell you to stop fucking her? Get to it. I'll be right back."

Aarav did as he was told. He slid in and out of Sola with long glides that took him from nearly slipping free again to as deep as he could get. If he was going to be tortured, she should be too. Good thing the dozens of times they'd *practiced* this over the past several weeks had built up his endurance. Now he made it a game to see how long he could prolong her rapture before giving in to his own. Every session had allowed him to increase his personal best record.

It felt incredible to be able to please her. To give her endless orgasms. Cash had been a remarkable teacher. If nothing else, Aarav owed the man for that.

And just like that he was back, settling in again as the snick of a plastic cap cut through Aarav and Sola's soft sighs and the whisper of their skin gliding together.

Cash must have warmed the oil in his hands, turning it fully liquid to coat his fingers and drizzle it over Aarav's hole. Because next thing Aarav knew, Cash had progressed from massaging his entrance to applying pressure, a single finger burrowing through the tight rings of muscle there.

"Relax, Aarav." Sola petted his chest. "It will be easier if you let him in instead of fighting it."

He unclenched his jaw and focused on each stroke of his dick within her until his body quit resisting and Cash dipped inside.

"That's right," Cash murmured as he began to work his finger in time to Aarav's pumping into Sola.

As much as Aarav tried to keep things barely moving, he couldn't help but speed up a bit as each backward motion impaled him deeper on Cash before he embedded himself fully within Sola again. It was perfection. Or at least he thought so until Cash added a second finger, then began to spread them apart within him, stretching his ass.

As if that wasn't enough, Cash used his free hand to massage Aarav's balls, tugging them with precisely the right amount of pressure. Aarav's stride hitched, but he didn't dare disappoint either of his lovers, so he kept fucking and being fucked in return.

"You like this." Sola didn't ask. "That's good, Aarav. Take it."

Cash blew out a breath of his own then. "The two of you are going to kill me."

"No, we decided not to," Sola shot back, proving she had far more brain cells engaged in that moment than Aarav did.

"Then you'd better focus and come on your man," Cash told her. "I'm not going to fuck him until you do. Because although I'm usually pretty good at holding back, I don't think I'm going to be able to once I'm buried in him, driving you both into this bed."

Sola moaned at the thought.

"Come on, Aarav," Cash goaded him. "Fuck her so well she can't hold out on us. Get her off so we can quit screwing around and get down to business."

Aarav gritted his teeth, determined on doing what Cash demanded. He levered onto his arms and focused on the angle of his plunges within Sola so that the tip of his dick connected with her most sensitive places. He made sure to use every inch of what he had, allowing the ridge around the head of his cock to tug against the ring of muscles at her entrance before pumping into her balls-deep once more.

And when her breathing hitched and a sheen of perspiration began to develop on her chest, he dipped his head and bit the crook of her neck not so gently.

She gasped and shuddered beneath him. "Not fair."

"You can do it to me later." Aarav had to close his eyes for a moment to keep his resolution to hold out while he helped her let go. The thought of unleashing her wild side could wreck his poise and make him shoot on command.

That was not what they were going for.

Cash took pity on him and snaked his free hand around Aarav's hip so he could strum Sola's clit in time to Aarav's motions and the coordinated insertion of his own fingers deep into Aarav's ass.

"She's getting close," Cash practically purred. "When she loses it, you're going to make sure to stuff her full of your cock and stay in, but don't fucking come."

His dirty talk triggered Sola. She threw her head back, leaving her neck wide open for Aarav to kiss and suck on. The faint purple marks he left behind spurred him to claim her, to fuse them more completely than ever before. On a level far beyond only the physical.

He tipped her chin down and stared straight into her

eyes as he hammered into her furiously for a few strokes before resuming his careful attack on her g-spot when the quick, intense motions proved too much for them both. With the added stimulation of Cash's fingers, Aarav was walking a fine line between restraint and indulgence.

Sola shattered. She trapped Cash's hand between her and Aarav as she arched upward.

"Go deep and stay still," Cash told Aarav.

When Aarav feared he'd gone too far, risked too much, and couldn't resist the tugging of Sola's pussy around his cock, Cash made his move.

He shifted quickly, withdrawing his hands from both Sola and Aarav, then set his cock at the entrance to Aarav's body and tucked inside.

Aarav yelped. Not in pain, since Cash slipped along his lubricated and stretched passage, but in surprise. The intense sensation, with—yes—a hint of discomfort, pulled him back from the brink of climax.

He was filled with wonder and joy and a sense of fulfillment he'd never experienced before.

This was where he was meant to be, a conduit between his lovers, being thrilled by them both, and giving them something equally pleasurable in return.

Sola hummed and stretched beneath him as the most powerful waves of her orgasm subsided only for Cash to set them off again by rocking them both when he began to move within Aarav.

Aarav's strangled groan made Sola laugh, her pure delight ringing around them.

All the depictions of sex Aarav had ever seen in the movies hadn't prepared him for how damn much fun it was to share this experience with these people and enjoy it on so many different levels.

The fullness of Cash heavy in his ass, which only got better each time the guy stroked Aarav's prostate. The pressure of Sola's pussy smothering his cock. The bliss smoothing out the stress lines in her face and Cash's heavy breath on his shoulder promising they'd done a damn fine job of distracting him from the shit show his life had turned into recently.

Aarav turned back, awed by the graceful yet commanding invasion Cash led as he pistoned in and out of Aarav's body, the motion turning Aarav into an extension of him to keep making love to Sola as well. Cash smiled, then captured Aarav's lips in a potent kiss that had Aarav clamping down on Cash and reaching deeper into Sola's pussy than ever before.

When he thought for sure he was going to crack and spill into Sola, ending their playtime, Cash broke free, but only to lean forward a bit more and make out with Sola too. The shift of his weight drove him deeper into Aarav, who saw stars.

Not only because his entire body vibrated with escalating ecstasy, but also because he could feel the connection between them growing stronger by the second. If he closed his eyes, he swore he could see energy flowing between them. But maybe that was just Cash and Sola fucking his brains out.

Cash clasped Aarav's hips, his thumbs pressed right above Aarav's crack. He sank to the root, then locked there, embedded fully in Aarav's ass. Then he looped one arm around Aarav's chest, holding him tightly so Aarav could feel the pounding of Cash's heart against his back before using Aarav to slam into Sola.

Aarav would never have treated her so roughly. Would

have been afraid to unshackle the primal parts of himself that Cash was taunting to come to the surface.

But she loved every moment and showed him by trying to wrap her legs around them both and fuse the three of them together. He wasn't going to complain as both of his lovers pawed at him, pulling them closer together.

He'd never felt something as incredible as being surrounded by them, attached to the two people he'd come to care most about in the world.

Suspended between them, he let them use him to delight each other and themselves.

"Sola...tell me you're with us." Cash's voice was strained, near to breaking. Was he emotional or merely clinging to the last of his ridiculous self-restraint? What would he do if she wasn't?

Aarav didn't find out.

"I don't want to fall alone this time." Sola looked straight up at Aarav. "Never again."

"I'm here" was all he could say.

Cash let go of Aarav then, unleashing him on them both. "Fuck us, Aarav. Make this happen for us all."

Aarav went wild. He bottomed out in Sola's pussy before backing up on Cash's cock. He was filled to capacity, his heart and his ass completely packed. He fucked them in a flurry of short jabs when he couldn't decide which direction was more pleasurable. It was a dead tie.

And in the end, both were miraculous, setting the bar for his sex life so high he wasn't sure he could ever top it.

Sola reached for him, dipping a finger into his mouth. He nipped it, setting her off. She screamed and came again, her orgasm powerful enough to ricochet through every nerve ending on his dick and down to his balls, which gathered before pumping every drop of come in them into her body.

The clamp of his ass on Cash's cock proved impossible for the other man to resist. As Aarav flooded Sola's pussy, Cash's come painted his insides.

Cash slid his hands beneath Aarav's arms and cupped his shoulders from underneath, pinning him in place as Cash spent every last bit of his strength and arousal on giving Aarav what he'd asked for.

They filled the room with their cries of conquest and triumph before they tipped to the side and melted into the mattress, their limbs still intertwined.

Full of awe and gratitude, Aarav's heart felt like it might burst.

Terrified of repeating the errors he'd made with Sola, and while still riding the high of endorphins and whatever other chemicals Sola and Cash had infused him with, Aarav blurted, "I love you. Both of you."

"I love you too," Sola was quick to respond despite her winded breathing as she snuggled close to him.

But instead of echoing their sentiments, Cash cleared his throat and glanced around the room as if searching for the exit.

Their satisfied glow morphed instantly into something awkward.

"Sorry. I went too far," Aarav backpedaled. "It was a reflex. That's all. I get that you see sex differently than me and being with us is only a temporary situation for you. I didn't mean to make things weird. Thanks for, uh, helping me out with...that."

Sola clung to Aarav, as if trying to love him double to

make up for Cash pulling away. She shot a questioning stare at Cash.

"It's...a lot right now. To imagine that could be possible. Like...how? I'm processing everything." Cash rubbed his temples and backed away from them to the foot of the bed as if he regretted what they'd done now that his boner had been appeased. They'd tried their hardest to prove he was worthy of their love. But they'd failed. "Is it okay if I crash in the guest room tonight?"

Aarav tried to give him the benefit of the doubt. The meeting with his father must still be screwing with his head. But after he'd bared himself so completely, literally and figuratively, it was tough to deal with Cash's rejection.

"Stay," Sola urged at the same time Aarav spoke.

"Of course. Go," he said, his permission sounding mechanical even to him as some of his robotic tendencies returned a little too late to shield his heart.

"My whole world is imploding and being rebuilt and nothing is like I expected it to be." Cash's stare flicked between Aarav and Sola. "Maybe it's going too fast. I feel out of control and overwhelmed. Like I can't breathe."

Sola did a partial crunch as if preparing to go to him and offer him comfort, but Cash slipped off the end of the bed. He shook his head. "I need some space. Please."

She dropped her hand and let him go. Aarav sure as shit wasn't about to beg when Cash had made it clear that he hadn't found the balm he'd needed in the intimacy they'd just shared. Maybe because it had been about sex alone for Cash instead of the soul-altering expression of affection and togetherness Aarav had thought it felt like to him.

Well, shit.

Cash retreated, taking a few strides backward before

spinning on his heel and heading out the door, leaving Sola and Aarav staring at each other in as much shock as if someone had dumped a bucket of ice water on the white-hot glow they'd generated together.

"I'm so sorry, Aarav." She captured his face between her palms, her fingers stroking his cheeks and down to his beard. "I know what that meant to you. If he can't see it too, then fuck him."

"Hey, it's okay. Give him some time." Aarav tried to understand even when his guts had turned to lead. "And if this isn't what he wants, then it's better to find out now."

"No. It would have been right to say so before he took something you only would give to someone important to you." Sola stopped short of saying the L word again.

"Whether or not he feels the same, he'll always be special to me. And to you too." Aarav appreciated her loyalty more than he could put into words, but despite the pain lancing him...the truth was, he had come to care deeply about Cash in the brief but intense time they'd spent together. And whether or not they'd fucked first, it would have ripped his heart out to say goodbye.

So at least he'd gotten to experience this once before everything fell apart.

Because he didn't know how it would work with him and Sola if Cash wasn't there, and his ghost would serve as a constant reminder that Aarav had failed Sola and cost her the rapture she'd found between them. Having experienced it himself, he knew what a devastating loss that would be.

Suddenly, he could hardly swallow. He needed something to drink. *His tea.*

He groaned.

"Are you okay?" Sola asked quietly, her concern only

making him feel worse about ruining the good thing she'd had going.

"Fine." Aarav rolled from bed, marched into the kitchen, and dumped the ruined tea down the drain. He should have known better than to trust someone else with something so important to him.

The liquid was so dark it was nearly black. Far too strong to be palatable.

Maybe I'm too much—too much work, too much fuss.

And it had gone cold long ago, before he even had a chance to enjoy it.

Maybe Cash is too bitter and too gun-shy to accept that he's found not only one person who adores him exactly as he is, but two of them.

Aarav couldn't unsteep the tea any more than he could take back the powerful emotions that had inspired him to push the boundaries of their intimacy faster than Cash had apparently been able to handle.

Aarav threw his mug into the sink hard enough that it shattered. He stood there staring at the shards of his favorite cup as blood tricked down his knuckles, wondering how he was going to keep himself together and if he alone could ever be enough for Sola again, now that she'd developed a taste for being shared.

He cursed himself for surrendering to unwise urges and allowing himself to feel so damn much. Because right then it hurt like hell.

16

———————

The next morning Cash sat on the side of Aarav's guest bed with his head in his hands, wondering why he'd gotten so twisted up the moment Aarav took their liaison beyond casual sex. It wasn't like what he'd shared with Sola and Aarav had anything in common with the meaningless fucks he'd indulged in his entire adult life.

He curled his bare toes in the area rug that warmed up the gorgeous dark wood floor. Even the houseplants staged around the room in distressed bronze pots made him feel comfortable and at home in a way nothing but the sea had before.

If he was being honest, what he'd loved about living on the ocean was that he was insulated from disappointment and the people who would wound him if given half a chance. Like his father.

Here, he didn't worry about that because everyone was accepting. He knew more than his body was safe inside those walls. Or at least he had right up until the moment

Aarav's pledge reminded him that they'd reached a place where if it didn't work out, it could destroy him.

Whether they'd said the words or not, their coming together had already transformed him. And in the moment Aarav and Sola had needed the same reassurance from him, he'd let them down. Shit.

He had to find them and hope they'd give him a second chance.

Before he could rise to seek them out, a loud triple-bang rattled the door. It was Sola, who was probably even more pissed at him than Aarav considering how protective they were of each other. "Cash, get your ass up. Meeting downstairs and you're coming with. Everyone will be there, so there's no one else to babysit you. Let's go. Right now unless you want me to let Jordan throw you in the basement after all."

Oh fuck. Yup. She was pissed.

He was still hopping on one foot across the living room as he dragged his second sock on when Aarav and Sola, their expressions steely, emerged from Aarav's bedroom.

"First, can I just say—"

"We don't have time for that." Sola had her business face on. She didn't even look him in the eye when she breezed past and headed out the door to call the elevator. Marcus, Kennedy, and Knox had beat them to it and were waiting impatiently as he joined them, Aarav bringing up the rear.

When the elevator dinged and the doors slid open, the car was already jam-packed. Ruby, Liam, Ace, Legend, Tavish, and Nolan were inside. Ace tucked Ruby between him and Liam, probably not accidentally, before waving them in. "Hurry, squish in. We can make it in one trip."

Damn, there really must be something urgent breaking.

Cash shifted awkwardly to keep from plastering up against either Sola or Aarav when they so clearly were not having his bullshit that morning. As desperately as he wanted to blurt out an apology, there was no way he was going to let all these badasses know he'd done something idiotic and upset their friends. Then he'd be taking a trip to the basement for sure. Even if he hoped to set things to rights as soon as possible.

The band of Shields marched to the command center together, taking their places. Cash glanced over his shoulder at the door, wondering if he was really welcome.

"Sit." Sola didn't look at him when she issued the command.

He cleared his throat, rehearsing something better to say than simply sorry, when Jordan joined them and took his seat at the head of the table.

"We have an opening. We need to act fast." Jordan nodded to Ruby, who put up a map, some pictures of what looked like an arid landscape of reddish soil and sporadic gnarled trees along with a rusted out truck abandoned on the side of an extremely rural road on the main curved screen. "During the video call with Mr. Kalykalaos, Ruby hacked his phone and has been using the backdoor access she planted to get us a shit ton of information, including ongoing transmissions of all his conversations via calls, emails, and texts."

"You're welcome." She tossed her bright hair over her shoulder and grinned.

"It turns out, our conversation might have convinced him of how fucked he really is." Jordan grimaced. "But instead of reconsidering our offer, that dumbass set up a meeting with Jay Barber himself. This isn't some mid-tier lackey. He's the top piece of shit. At least until someone else takes him out and steals his spot. That's how this usually goes."

Cash sighed, and though Sola's jaw twitched, she didn't so much as glance in his direction, never mind offer her hand or rub his back. He hadn't realized until right then that he'd come to rely on those simple gestures for comfort. This might easily turn out to be one of the worst days of his life.

Like his father, he had no one to blame but himself.

"Any clues about why?" Nolan asked.

"We think he's going to try to negotiate his way out of their partnership." Jordan shrugged one shoulder.

"Wow. That *is* stupid." Ace shook his head. Liam smacked him with the back of his hand. "Oof. Sorry, Cash."

"Runs in the family." Cash pinched the bridge of his nose, making Aarav crack and peek over, though only for a moment.

"There's no way that's going to work, is there?" Marcus tried for a bit more tact as he asked Jordan.

"Absolutely not." Jordan's mouth formed a slash straight across his face. "Not under normal circumstances and especially not because we're going to take this opportunity to wipe Jay Barber off the face of the planet before he can ruin anyone else's life. That's not going to make his organization especially pleased with Mr. Kalykalaos."

A numbness started spreading from the pit of Cash's stomach outward until even his lips buzzed. He knew what they were saying. His father was doomed. Had been since he hung up on Jordan. So why didn't that upset him?

At least they were only using his name and not referring to him as Cash's dad. Because he realized then, the man who'd sired him had never truly been that to him.

"How are we going to do this?" Aarav wondered.

Jordan sat up straighter. "That's what we're here to discuss. There are some...complications."

"Why is it never fucking easy?" Legend grumbled.

"Like what?" Levi asked.

"For starters..." Jordan held up one finger. "It's a mobile meeting because Jay Barber is paranoid as fuck about being ambushed at a static location."

"In fairness, it's not paranoia if we're out to end him," James chirped.

"Valid point." Jordan raised another finger. "The route he'll be taking is one he travels often through northern Africa from his base city to his hometown in the middle of fucking nowhere. It's along that road on screen where there's absolutely zero cover, which is probably why he regularly ignores his security team's advice and drives himself in a standard vehicle when he goes there. That and pure arrogance. He hasn't been challenged in the past twelve years. Luckily for us, he's getting over confident."

Jordan gestured toward the 3D model Ruby was displaying for them. Cash could see how that flat terrain would make it impossible for someone to hide.

"Because of that," Jordan continued, "Ruby was able to use Mr. Kalykalaos's credentials to wiggle into their systems and then together with JRad from OSPD, they busted the cartel's network wide open. Turns out they were evading law enforcement so long because they scan for heat signatures in front of Jay Barber's vehicle on all trips. Anyone out there would be—and have been in the past—a sitting duck."

Cash winced, finally understanding how evil the dealings his father had supported really were. Government agents, soldiers, people who tried to make the world a better place like every one of the Shields surrounding him now had sacrificed their own lives to try to stop it.

He prayed they could pull it off this time.

"So you're saying we can't ship Aarav over there to take out the trash for us." Nolan fixed his already perfect hair, which always made him seem like a real-life action figure to Cash.

"Exactly." Jordan shook his head. "It's too dangerous, even from a distance. Guns are their business. They know where to look. So who has ideas? Shout them out."

"We take a ride ourselves coming from the opposite direction. And when we pass them...*boom!*" Tavish's dramatization startled Cash, making him jump.

Jordan shared an empathetic glance with him. "A possibility, but one I think they'll be prepared for. It has some flaws. I don't think there's a high probability of bringing our team home in one piece afterward and it would also mean Mr. Kalykalaos goes too."

"Are we trying to protect him?" Ransom asked.

"If at all possible." Jordan nodded once. "He'll spend a long time in jail, but it's better than dead. And maybe there's more information he can give us to help if he has a change of heart."

"He won't." Cash knew his father well enough to say that with one-hundred percent certainty.

"Air strike," Sola proposed.

"Won't work." Ruby tapped away, zooming the satellite

images in on hunks of metal with long tubes sticking out placed around the area. "Artillery. They take out any planes not cleared to fly over their turf."

Jesus. Cash had never realized there were people like this out there in the world. He'd been sheltered and spoiled and naïve.

"I know we're not done with our final rounds of testing, but..." Aarav stroked his beard. "Is this a job for the DeathBot project?"

Jordan opened his mouth, but there weren't any objections to counter whatever the hell Aarav had suggested.

Aarav got up and circled the table until he could examine the area more closely. "I thought I saw... Yes. Right there."

He pointed to the rusted-out powder-blue truck that had obviously been abandoned years ago, if not decades. Something Jay Barber and his team would ignore, having passed it millions of times before. "We put it in the bed of this truck and cover it with some of that dry brush that's everywhere. It will look like it blew in there."

"That has potential." Jordan beamed at Aarav. "And you feel confident the kinks are worked out? The delay issue we were having?"

Aarav looked to Ruby then. She nodded. "So long as he stays here and is hardwired into our systems, I can make sure we have the resources to make it happen like we've been practicing."

"I don't know. You'd be half the world away, taking a kill shot through—an admittedly, very sophisticated— remote-controlled gun." Jordan tapped his lips.

"It'll be just like playing video games." Ace grinned. "Have you ever seen the man destroy us in *Call of Duty*?

We quit inviting him to game night because it's no fun for anyone else."

It sounded like something out of a sci-fi movie to Cash. That they had the technology and Aarav had the skills to even consider something like that both impressed and terrified him.

Jordan nodded. "You're right. This is our best shot."

James chuckled. "You're so punny, Jordan."

He ignored James, though the corner of his mouth quirked up. "Sola, you're going to lead the operation on the ground. You've had the best instincts about this case and I need you to see it through."

She perked up. "Of course. Thank you."

"Besides, you're the only person Aarav lets touch his *rifle*," Ruby teased, drawing a laugh from everyone around the table.

Aarav, however, tensed, making Cash wish he had the right to comfort the man. The idea of Sola putting herself in grave danger—*again*—because of his own damn father infuriated Cash.

"Liam, Tavish, and Legend, you're with Sola. Kennedy, go along with them, but stay with the jet in case they need medical support. Marcus and Knox, we'll also need you to guard the jet, Kennedy, Aven, and the rest of the flight crew. Just in case."

"On it, boss." Marcus tugged on his ear, making the large diamond in its lobe sparkle.

"I hate to throw one last wrench in there." Ruby popped up a world clock with their current location and that of the operation along with the sunrise and sunset times. A countdown timer appeared, taking up one full half of the panel, giving Cash greater anxiety with every second that disappeared. "There's hardly enough time to make it there and assemble this thing under cover of night."

"I know." Jordan cleared his throat. "It's my fault. I went over every detail we learned myself, multiple passes, to make sure there are no fucking errors. Jay Barber is the evil bastard we want. And I swear to you, I will never give any of you the wrong target again."

That was enough for the team.

"See you later." Sola stood fast enough that her chair rolled away. Liam, Tavish, and Legend weren't far behind. Marcus, Kennedy, and Knox moved as one, joining the rest of the agents.

"Sola, I—" Cash had no idea what he was going to say, only that he needed her to know how much he cared, even if he hadn't been able to accept it the night before.

James reached over and touched Cash's forearm, silencing him with a gentle squeeze. "She doesn't have time and you really shouldn't distract her right now. Whatever is causing you three those bags under your eyes will have to wait."

Cash snapped his jaw closed at that. He couldn't stand the thought of being responsible for stealing her focus from her mission and returning safely to Shields where he could hash things out with her...and Aarav...later.

Aarav stayed glued to his seat as if he too had lots he wanted to say but couldn't. Sola peered over her shoulder and caught his expression. She jogged back and bent down to kiss him, full on the lips, in front of all their friends. Despite the circumstances, Cash's cock twitched in his jeans. "You have to trust me to do my job. I know how to fend for myself. It's not any different because we sleep together these days. Don't worry. I'm going to take great care of your *gun*. You just worry about getting the shot off."

Then she was gone, disappearing into the hallway with her hair streaming behind her as she caught up with the rest of the team heading for the airfield.

Aarav swallowed hard, blinked a few times, then pointedly ignored Cash as he strode past him to Ruby's station. "Can you scan the area into our simulation software so we can run through this a few hundred times before we try it for real?"

"Already did it." Ruby tapped a few things, then handed Aarav a joystick and a headset. As soon as he put them on, he was transported to another continent. Far out of Cash's reach.

James flashed Cash an empathetic smile. "Come on. You can hang out with me the rest of the day. I want to hear all about how you fucked this up when things were going so well. I'll help you figure out how to pull your head out of your very fine ass."

Cash couldn't believe it, but he laughed, because he believed James just might have the answers and he was willing to do anything to get Aarav and Sola back.

17

———

Aarav swiped the headset from his aching skull. He blinked as his eyes adjusted to the lighting in the command center and remembered how to focus on something right in front of him rather than far away, even if that distance was a very fancy illusion.

"You've got this," Ruby reassured him. "The simulation includes the most likely predicted wind and weather forecast, and I promise you it's entirely accurate. You haven't missed in the last hundred run-throughs at least."

"Yeah, but real life has a way of being far more unpredictable." Aarav hated the idea of Sola—and the rest of her team—out there, risking everything to give him a single shot at success.

"Rather than sit here until you burn yourself out, you'd be better off getting something to eat, shaking out those knots in your muscles, and maybe..."

"What?" He hoped she didn't recommend a power nap because there was no way he would be able to doze off with this much anticipation amping him up.

"If you don't think it will fuck up your head, maybe

talk to Cash. I realize it's none of my business, except that I want to see you happy, but it seemed like there was some heavy shit left unsaid between you earlier."

"I think I already said too much, actually. I told him and Sola that I love them." Aarav felt like a moron for it too. Not because it was untrue, but because he should have known that not everyone was like him. In fact, most people didn't have to have that level of affection for someone as a prerequisite to finding them attractive. It didn't have the same implications when most people shared a good time together.

He needed to remember that.

"I mean this in the nicest way possible, Aarav." Ruby drew a deep breath, then rolled her eyes. "But...no shit."

"It seemed to shock Cash." Getting it off his chest eased the tension making his fingers wobble the slightest bit. And given what he needed to do—soon now, he glanced at the jet's progress as it prepared to land—that was a welcome relief.

"He's had a rough couple of weeks. Lots of change. Give him a minute to absorb it all." Ruby smiled softly. "He dropped off a thermos and sandwiches he made for us about fifteen minutes ago."

Aarav perked up. "Tea?"

"I'm guessing it is. And don't get all pissy if he only used fifty-seven leaves instead of fifty-eight. He's trying and it's pretty damn cute."

"I'm not *that* particular." Aarav frowned.

"Could have fooled me." Ruby bumped her shoulder into his. "Just teasing, Aarav. Well, except about the relationship stuff."

"Noted." Aarav popped open the lid on the thermos and breathed deep of the scented steam before nearly searing his lips and tongue on the freshly brewed tea. "Mmm. Perfection."

Then he did as Ruby had suggested, stretching in between deep pulls on the travel mug and bites of the sandwich left beside it. It had two slices of gouda, a layer of greens, and a single slice of turkey with a smear of mayo and a hint of black pepper. Precisely how he liked it.

Ruby went back to monitoring the team's progress. When Aarav had finished, she looked at him. "They're on the ground. You ready for me to call everyone in here? You want me to tell James to bring Cash or to have him wait in one of our holding pens?"

Aarav winced. There was no denying Cash had cooperated from the moment they'd abducted him. He deserved to see how things went down. Truth was, Aarav liked having him near, even if Cash wasn't ready to accept that yet. "Yeah. Let's go. Cash too."

It only took a moment from when Ruby summoned them for the Shields to reassemble in the command center. Aarav stayed at his station beside Ruby, unwilling to alter anything at all from their practice sessions. She tensed the instant Liam appeared on the comms feed, before glancing over at Ace, who gripped the arm of his chair with his good hand.

This web of links between them was what made their team so strong, but it was also a weakness. Because caring was terrifying. In that moment, Aarav realized he might have been the emotionless shell they'd accused him of, but only to protect himself. And those days had ended the moment he allowed Sola—and now Cash—into his heart.

His breath caught in his chest when Sola bounded from the jet, sending up a puff of that dry orangey dust that reminded him of a Martian landscape. For all he was able to help her now, she might as well have been on the other side of the galaxy.

She had been exactly right. He had to have faith in her skills and abilities and their training or he would lose his shit. He risked a glance at Cash, who'd taken the chair closest to Aarav and noted the grooves around the guy's eyes and mouth. Whether it was to reassure himself or Cash, Aarav said quietly, "She's really good at her job. She's going to be fine."

Cash nodded but didn't peel his eyes from the screen where the team was stretching out between the jet and the SUV parked nearby. They started a chain, handing each other the heavy pieces of the disassembled DeathBot, working as quickly and efficiently as possible.

James kept a calm and steady stream of communication flowing to the team, letting them know how much time there was remaining until first light as they raced along the utterly empty roads. If they were spotted now, they would be in trouble. There was nowhere to hide and even the four of them, heavily armed, were no match for the gunrunners, who would far outnumber them and have endless supplies.

This—not the shot Aarav was still recalculating endlessly in his mind—was the part he was most worried about. He knew Sola would set his equipment up as meticulously as Cash made his tea, but didn't know how he'd survive if she died doing it.

The command center was absolutely silent, a miracle for the gaggle of Shields remaining at headquarters. Jordan switched his comms so only they could hear and assigned a couple people to each of the field operatives. "Don't take your eyes off your buddies as they assemble, mount, and level this thing. Make sure every step matches what we've practiced exactly. Call it out if you see something that doesn't add up."

Aarav was usually out there with them, covering them from afar. It was odd to be safely enshrined in the office, but comforting to know that they had his back in the field even as he had the rest of the team's.

"We're running four minutes behind." James frowned as Tavish and Legend struggled to bolt the DeathBot to the rusted metal of the truck bed. It was massive and heavy as fuck. It had to be properly secured or it could shift. Even a few millimeters were too many when Aarav needed to rotate the barrel of the gun with his remote control. "First light in less than six. Come on. Come on."

Ruby interjected, her voice going out to the team in the field as well as the Shields at home. "We've got a tractor approaching from the west. Fucking farmer's early this morning. You're going to have to be out of there in two minutes and seventeen seconds before he crests the hill and spots you."

Liam flew from the truck bed and began gathering brush. He used some to obscure their tracks while covering the parts of the DeathBot they'd finished.

Sola joined Tavish and Legend, brandishing the hammer drill like she was part of James's Powertools crew rather than the Shields. James gave her step-by-step instructions and when she got the damn thing in place, Tavish confirming it with a tug that didn't budge the base, James said, "Nice work. I'm sure Devon will hire you if this Shields thing doesn't work out for you. Now get the hell out of there."

Sola planted one hand on the side of the truck bed, then vaulted over it to the backside of the truck, making sure their tracks were as discreet as possible as they chose their path back to their ride.

They piled inside and made it onto the road, where they drove sedately in the opposite direction of the approaching farmer. If he noticed their taillights vanishing down the country lane, he'd have no reason to suspect they were anything but a local or a random car passing through.

"How the fuck do you do this?" Cash's ragged exhale cut through the room. He clutched his chest and bent over as the rest of the team celebrated with whoops, high fives, and even a sedate smile from Jordan.

Aarav felt better already, knowing Sola and her unit were about to be safely ensconced in the jet with Marcus, and Knox for additional firepower. They'd agreed the team would stay on the ground until the rest of the mission was complete in case something went off the rails and they needed to step in. Or maybe, Aarav hoped for Cash's sake, if his father changed his mind and decided to accept Jordan's protection.

The team had barely boarded when Ruby spoke up. "We've got movement on Mr. Kalykalaos's phone. He's leaving the hotel, heading toward Jay Barber's estate."

Aarav kept his hand laid flat on his jeans-clad thighs, unwilling to ball them up and let his fingers get sweaty. But nearly an hour later, he was resorting to meditation techniques including breath control to remain as impassive as this shot would require him to be.

The celebratory atmosphere that had followed the successful completion of phase one of the operation was replaced with anxiety about the second stage.

"Time to gear up," Ruby told him as she tracked the flashing red dot of Cash's father's cellphone signal across the map. "You should have the first visual of the car in under three minutes and be in range in four minutes and seventeen seconds for a total of thirty-nine seconds based on their current speed. Looks like they've got cruise control on, and haven't accelerated or braked since they left the city. The wind is currently five knots from the south and is being updated in real time on your heads-up display. Based on our earlier simulations, this gives you a ninety-six percent chance of success."

Aarav nodded, then slipped on his headset and flipped down the visor, which was also his display screen. He didn't relish the knowledge he was about to take someone's life, but he reminded himself of the images of the slaughtered innocents in the market square and his hands were steady on the controls.

The rest of the room went silent around him. He wasn't wearing comms so he couldn't hear Sola and her team or anything beyond the command center.

He counted in his mind until the car was due to arrive in three...two...

The instant he spotted it, through the enhanced scope of the DeathBot, he knew something was drastically wrong. "*Fuck!*"

"Tell me," Jordan commanded.

"Jay Barber isn't driving." Ruby must have displayed the visual input onto the massive command center screen because hushed exclamations zipped around the room behind Aarav.

"My father is?" Cash sounded confused. He hadn't realized what this meant yet.

"I'm on the wrong side of the road." Aarav's guts turned to lead and beads of sweat spontaneously formed on the back of his neck.

"Forty-four seconds until they're in range," Ruby reminded them. There wasn't time to think or to make a new plan.

"You can still get the shot?" Jordan asked Aarav.

"Yes, but not without collateral damage." Aarav mentally calculated the caliber of the bullet and how much energy it would likely have after smashing the car glass. Still plenty to pass through one human and into another.

"Do it." Jordan gave the order Aarav would have been fine with in any other circumstance.

"Twenty seconds," Ruby said.

Aarav flipped up the goggles on his mask and whipped his gaze to Cash's. "Will you hate me if I kill your father?"

Cash's gloriously bronzed skin turned deathly pale.

"Ten."

"I can't do this, Jordan." Aarav felt like he might be sick.

"The needs of the many outweigh the needs of one. Even when that one is you. Or Cash. Or his father." Jordan didn't raise his voice. And Aarav knew he was right.

He regretted that he wasn't actually the cyborg they'd accused him of being so often. He wished he wasn't swimming in doubt and fear and grief of what he'd lost before he'd even really had it.

"In range. For thirty-seven seconds."

Aarav flipped the visor back down and was prepared to do his duty. He set the crosshairs perfectly and tracked the car, sure that if he so much as twitched, he would accomplish his mission. He took a deep breath and prepared to do it. Until he imagined having to face Sola and apologize for destroying her dreams and her soul as surely as his own once she got home.

"Twenty seconds."

He could have taken the shot ten times over by then. And still he didn't.

Was a chance at love—if Cash even could be convinced he wanted that—worth losing his job, betraying his team, and letting an evil piece of shit continue to wreck untold lives?

"The window is closing in ten...nine..."

"Aarav." Jordan practically growled. "He was warned."

James even added quietly, "It's the right thing to do."

"Five...four..."

Aarav would never know for sure what he had decided, because just then a warm and familiar hand covered his. The additional weight caused him to relax. His palm lowered a fraction of an inch. And together, they solved a problem for the world.

The bullet flew through the air, true to its course. The driver's side window of the vehicle shattered and the mixed blood and gore of both occupants splattered the passenger's side. The car slowed, though not much, before it veered from the road and flew down the embankment, rolling at least twenty times before coming to a stop upside-down, its wheels spinning aimlessly in the air.

The caravan of security team members and other associates from Jay Barber's enterprise screeched to a halt, making them easy pickings. If being part of Shields had taught Aarav anything, it was that the supply of bad guys willing to fill the shoes the Shields emptied was far greater than that of the heroes.

He funneled his terror and delayed the inevitable—

seeing the death of his own dreams in Cash's eyes—by staying inside his headset. "Permission to clean up?"

"Absolutely." Jordan nodded. "We're not going to have a better chance to make a difference than right now."

Aarav unleashed everything pent up inside him, taking shots with shocking speed and accuracy, even for him. He resented every last one of those bastards who'd put him in this impossible predicament and wouldn't have hesitated for an instant to take him out had the situation been reversed.

"Damn. Remind me never to piss you off." Ace grunted as if someone, likely Ruby, had smacked him.

It took less time than brewing his beloved tea. With one final bullet between the shoulder blades of someone trying to escape the repercussions of their heinous decisions, it was over. Then there wasn't a hint of motion remaining in that cursed valley, unless the shifting drifts of terra cotta colored dust, streaked with rivulets of blood counted.

Aarav ripped off the headset and tossed it aside, his breathing going from measured to ragged as he sucked in uneven breaths.

"We done with this?" Ruby double-checked.

Jordan said, "Yep. Get rid of it."

Moments later, the DeathBot performed its final task, blowing itself to smithereens so that anyone who came behind couldn't either injure themselves with it or reverse engineer its technology and sell it to their enemies. Rocks and clouds of dust obliterated the camera feed. The signal glitched before the screen blanked out.

"Oopsies." James tapped the side of his head as if trying to reengage his comms. "Looks like Liam might have gone a little overboard with those explosives."

"Better to make sure it's gone." Jordan didn't seem to mind.

Aarav turned to Ruby. "Can you get Sola for me? I need to talk to her. To hear her voice." So that he could tell if it was tinged with resentment or disgust.

"Sorry. The shockwave from the DeathBot seems to have fucked the satellite connection. Everyone's fine. Aven radioed in before takeoff." Ruby clicked a few keys, then displayed several concentric neon green circles with a line moving through them like the second hand on a clock. One green blob progressed across the area. "Here's a feed from the local radar tower. There's our team. They're on their way home."

"Did you hear her react at all to..."

Ruby winced. "She cursed, then sounded like she was holding back tears. I could hear Kennedy consoling her before we lost our connection. I'm sorry. It's going to be a long seven hours, huh?"

Everyone knew, Sola wasn't prone to overreaction. Even if Cash forgave him, would Sola? He figured their chances had died along with everyone in that cursed valley.

Aarav's shoulders slumped. "Very."

But there was one thing he could do with that time. And that was face Cash. Figure out where they stood at least so that when Sola rejoined them, he had some sort of plan.

He'd beg forgiveness from them both if it would do a damn thing.

Aarav counted to five, then looked up at Cash, who had sunk back into his seat at their table, his face buried in his hands. James was leaning over, squeezing his shoulder, but it didn't seem like Cash even realized the other man was there.

So Aarav moved closer, afraid of what he would see when Cash opened his eyes.

He crouched in front of Cash, the rest of the team giving them the illusion of space and privacy by averting their gazes and pretending not to eavesdrop as they rehashed the mission.

"Are you okay?" That had to be the dumbest thing he'd ever asked someone.

Hell, even *he* wasn't really okay with the split-second decisions he'd been forced to make.

His fingers hovered over Cash's knee, then froze, wondering how the guy could possibly tolerate being touched by the same hand that had slaughtered his father.

"I will be. Someday." Cash swallowed hard. "It might take some time, though. Just like I said last night. I'm sorry if that hurt you."

"I'm the one who should be apologizing. For pressuring you and now...for this. Can you ever forgive me for murdering your father?"

"I thought we didn't use the M word around here." Was Cash actually making a joke?

James hid a snort with a terribly fake cough.

"And anyway, did you do it...or did I?" Cash tipped his head then, and Aarav wanted to lie. To promise it hadn't been Cash. But if he was going to have any chance at salvaging what he desired most, he had to do better than he had in the past and trust that the people he loved could handle their complicated emotions and that so could he.

"Honestly, I have no idea," Aarav admitted.

"It's probably for the best. But I wouldn't have held it against you if you'd gone ahead on your own." One of the knots in Aarav's intestines unkinked itself. "He had a chance to walk away, to do better. Truth is, you were right last night. He wasn't capable of that. Or maybe simply didn't want to do it."

"He wasn't able to care for you either. That's not a reflection on how deserving you are of love from other people. Like me. And Sola, if—between last night and now—I haven't fucked that up. There was something wrong with him, not you."

Cash nodded. "I'm starting to believe that even if it seems impossible."

Aarav hooked his hand behind Cash's neck even as Cash reached for him. They drew each other nearer until their mouths found each other. Aarav settled in to the slow, careful exchange without ever once taking his stare from Cash's.

It probably would have seemed inappropriate to people who didn't live their high-stakes lives, but Aarav and Cash provided welcome destressing for the rest of the team after their brutal work was over. They quit pretending not to notice Cash and Aarav making up and making out. Instead, they cheered them on with whistles and catcalls. Hell, James even snapped a picture.

It was only when they broke apart that Cash winced. "What can we do to make Sola less upset with us?"

"I have an idea." Aarav had thought about it over and over the night before and couldn't get the idea for a special gift out of his mind.

"Does it involve your tongues doing something other than wasting time talking?" Ruby asked with a perfectly arched brow. "Just saying. That might be the most effective approach."

Ace grinned at that. "Would that work on you, too? I'll let Liam know when he arrives."

Ruby flipped him off, but when she spun around to her workstation, she crossed her legs tightly and Aarav could see her in profile, blushing just a bit.

James cracked his knuckles, and Aarav figured their coordinator had identified and locked on to his next target for his matchmaking schemes.

\# 18

S ola stumbled as she reached for the back door to Shields.

"Hey, careful." Legend threw an arm in front of her like a soccer mom who'd braked too hard to keep her from slamming her face on the glass. "Did you get any sleep at all?"

"Not a damn minute." She groaned. All she had been able to think about was Cash, his grief, and what Aarav taking that shot had done to his psyche. Cash had already bailed on them after some of the most intense sex of her life. Who would he turn to for comfort when his lover was also the person who took his parent—no matter how imperfect—from him?

Not normally a crier, she'd bawled her eyes out for hours as Kennedy rocked her and the jet's busted satellite dish had tortured her with a far-too-long silence where her imagination had free rein to imagine the worst.

Cash would never forgive them.

For fuck's sake, he hadn't actually cared for them at all and had been trying to let them down easy the night before. How would she face both him and Aarav, who'd been forced to make such a horrible choice?

And would he still be willing to love her when she'd led him to emotional slaughter?

Sola was certain the impact of yesterday's shot would ricochet through their love life, tearing it to shreds long before she'd been ready for it to be ruined.

Liam opened the door to let her in while Tavish and Legend flanked her as they made their way to the bank of elevators. Missions like these brought them closer together, and their unspoken support was comfortable, if not quite as reassuring as Aarav's presence always was to her after they'd narrowly escaped danger.

This time the hazard was far more terrifying than anything physical.

She wasn't sure she could go back to feigning disinterest in Aarav or living next door to him, sharing a wall but not their lives. If this went as she expected, she might have to leave the only place she'd ever really belonged.

Sola was trembling by the time she rapped on Aarav's door.

Within moments, she heard the loud footfalls of someone sprinting for the door. Aarav yanked it open and stood there staring at her, his chest perfectly still as if he was holding his breath. Then it left him in a rush as if someone let all the air out of a giant balloon. "Can we talk?"

This was it. He was about to tell her it wasn't going to work. That she'd forced him out of his shell and he wasn't ready, might never be, to be so vulnerable. It was the moment when Cash would rail at them both, telling them how much he hated them for offing his piece of trash father.

This was the moment her dreams died.

Might as well get it over. Sola shrugged. "Sure."

So when he stepped back and she spied Cash hovering over his shoulder, a few feet back, she was a bit confused. He wasn't going after Aarav, wasn't screaming or accusing. None of that.

In fact, he had a new mug in his hand, similar in style to the one Aarav had smashed but a cheery blue color like the shallows off a Caribbean island rather than the pitch black of the ruined pottery that had dotted their sink a mere twenty-four hours before. "Do you want Aarav's tea? It looks like maybe you could use it more than him."

Sola tipped her head, confused by how mundane and homey the scene before her was compared to the nightmare scenarios she'd imagined on the ride home. Could Kennedy, Marcus, and Knox have had it right? They'd tried to console her, promising nothing was insurmountable when you loved each other. Those three certainly survived enough pain of their own on their path to happiness as a trio.

"I think I need something stronger. Got any whiskey?" she joked, though she wouldn't have turned down a shot or two to make whatever they needed to say to her more bearable.

Aarav glided the tips of his fingers over her cheeks, making her close her eyes while she leaned into his caress. She yelped when he scooped her into his arms and carried her into his living room, placing her on the couch between him and Cash. "Nah. I don't drink that stuff. But I think I have something you might like better."

He piqued Sola's interest, and her curiosity when

neither of the guys seemed awkward or angry with each other and focused on her instead.

Aarav gestured to a cube the size of a microwave on the ground, draped loosely and haphazardly with a blanket from the couch. What the hell was going on?

She whipped the cover from the object, half expecting it to be Cash's packed suitcase before he announced his return to his yacht. Instead, the most adorable, twitching pink nose stuck between the bars of a white wire cage. The bunny rabbit it was attached to blinked up at her with wide, innocent eyes.

"Who's this?" she asked as she flew to it and opened the hatch, sticking her hand in and gently stroking the fluffy, soft fawn colored fur.

"Meet Miss Nibbles." Aarav crouched behind Sola and started unbraiding her hair. He'd become obsessed with finger combing it and massaging her skull lately. She wasn't about to stop him when it felt so good, both to unwind around him and Cash and to let him take care of her.

Cash joined them, sitting on the floor as he plucked a piece of hay from the cage and fed it to the sweet animal. "I've never been jealous of a glorified rodent before."

Sola covered Miss Nibbles' floppy ears with her hands. "Shhh. Don't hurt her feelings."

Cash winced. "I'll try my best. I didn't mean to hurt yours or Aarav's either the other night."

A lump settled in Sola's throat. Cash was a good man. This was probably where he'd let them down easy before admitting he could never come to love the people who'd killed his father, no matter how much time or space they gave him to dissect what had happened and acclimate to them showering him with affection.

"I don't ever want you to leave angry again." Aarav added the press of his thumbs to the center of her neck, making her eyelids grow heavy. "Our jobs are too dangerous for that. Both because you shouldn't be preoccupied on the job and also because I never want the last thing we say to each other to be something we regret."

Cash nodded. "If nothing else, this has shown me that things can change, can be taken away in a heartbeat. So I don't want to waste any more time debating if this is possible with my brain when my soul already knows the answer."

Tears prickled Sola's eyes. Again. This time because joy overwhelmed her. They were saying things she couldn't make sense of unless they were about to make her wildest dreams come true.

"Miss Nibbles is yours," Aarav told her. "But we'd prefer it if she was ours, too."

Cash scooted forward so he could hold one of Sola's hands and one of Aarav's. "We have a bond. One that I want to explore. I've never met a single person as decent as both of you. When life throws hurdles in our path, I want to know I have two incredible humans like you to help me over it."

"If you want Miss Nibbles. Us. And a life together..." Aarav looked up at her from beneath his dark brows as if he wasn't sure how desperately she'd hoped this was how things could go when she got back.

It was impossible that Cash could forgive them.

That Aarav could allow them in.

And that she hadn't been too brazen to scare them both away.

She didn't let him finish. "I do!"

"Then accept our gift as a promise of the life we want

to build with you." Cash leaned over and kissed her cheek. "One where we can have all the things we were too afraid to believe possible until we met each other."

"I'm so sorry about your dad," Sola whispered, leaning her forehead on his.

"Me too. I wish he hadn't been so far gone..." Cash either didn't understand she'd been talking about them getting rid of the bastard, or he simply didn't agree it was something that merited an apology.

"And I'm sorry you had to make that impossible choice." She leaned against Aarav, tucking her head on his shoulder as Miss Nibbles licked her fingers.

Aarav looked her dead in the eyes. "I didn't. He did."

Cash shrugged. "In that moment, everything became crystal clear to me. I could be like him—ignoring the bigger picture in order to make life easier for myself—or I could try to be the man you two think you see in me. I choose you. I choose love."

Sola petted Miss Nibbles one last time, then lifted her from the cage and cuddled her close to her chest like Cash had Mr. Prickles when he'd been lost. She knew it had been that instant that she'd fallen for him. "The front door is locked, right?"

"Yeah, why?" Aarav gave her a questioning stare.

"Because Miss Nibbles doesn't deserve to be locked up." She set the bunny on the carpet and watched her hop around them excitedly before opening the side door to the enclosure so she could get back in if she needed a drink or preferred to lay in her comfy pile of hay. "She's safe here. Free to explore to her heart's content and be loved by not only me, but both of you too. She's the luckiest bunny in the world."

"Are we still talking about Miss Nibbles?" Cash asked as he tucked Sola's loose waves behind her ear.

"Each of us has escaped our own cage." Sola stood and held out her hands. Both of her guys took one and joined her as they made their way to the bedroom, careful not to disturb Miss Nibbles as she bounced around, her ears flopping as she celebrated her good fortune.

"Let me make up for last time." Cash hesitated on the threshold. "I trust you to take what you need from me and to give me your love in return."

"You have it, Cash." Aarav kissed first Sola, and then their lover.

And she knew they were about to have one spectacular welcome home party. Because sometimes, if you were willing to change just a little, you might discover all the things you thought were out of reach wind up clutched in your hands.

19

———

Cash had lost some things in the past twenty-four hours, but he'd also gained a hell of a lot. Clarity, about who he was and who he wanted to be. Confidence, about his place in this new world he'd found himself in. And compassion, for the issues each of them struggled with.

He was sure, now, that working on things together would give them the best chance at reaching their common goal—being loved in exactly the way that fulfilled each of them and made the hard times that would inevitably come from time to time that much easier to bear.

And the rest of their lives...well...they had plenty to look forward to.

Cash didn't shy away when Sola drew his T-shirt over his head while Aarav got rid of his light gray sweats. He stood before them, completely naked, waiting for them to take what they wanted and give him what he needed in return.

They kissed each other, their stress and worry from

195

the past few days morphing into passion that could find a physical outlet. If that's what he could do to help them, after this operation and the others that would come, he was plenty willing.

Cash speared the fingers of one hand into Aarav's hair and the other into Sola's, directing them to continue feasting on each other while his cock grew harder with every swipe of their tongues and clash of their lips.

While they amused each other, he got to work, stripping off their clothes until they were as exposed as he was, bared to each other in the full light of the promising day.

Sola reached for him, fishing for his dick while still making out with Aarav. Her fingers wrapped around his shaft and stroked, using the hold to draw him nearer, into their circle. Then she angled her head, breaking free. Her other hand mimicked the one pumping him up, doing the same to Aarav.

It wasn't going to take much, but both men let her play.

"Your turn." She nudged them together.

And when Aarav met Cash midway, Sola tugged them a bit until she could wrap both hands around them, capturing their erections in her two-fisted grip. Cash groaned when she held them together, his cock trapped against Aarav's, and began to stroke them simultaneously.

Aarav hissed, then sought Cash's mouth so he could continue to express his desire and prepare Cash for what was surely coming next. Sola bent over, her mouth opening as she fit just the tips of their hard-ons into it. She licked and teased as she continued to rub them from their bases to where her fingers met her lips.

She couldn't take much of them this way, but that was

for the best if he was going to have any chance of lasting long enough to satisfy both her and Aarav.

Aarav shot him a glance along with a strangled moan that clearly communicated he was in tune with Cash. So they took a step back and went into action. Cash turned toward Sola and picked her up. His hands clasped her tight ass as she wrapped her legs around him, their bodies aligning so perfectly that he could have slipped inside her and fucked her standing right there in the middle of their bedroom if he hadn't had other plans.

He placed her sideways on the bed, her head right on the edge. And when he knelt with one knee on either side of her so he could bury his face in her pussy and get her ready to take them, she didn't waste the opportunity to inhale him deep into her mouth in a single stroke.

"Damn." He sank lower, feeding her more of him, leaving himself entirely wide-open to Aarav, who watched them from where he stood planted to the floor as if admiring a masterpiece in a museum instead of his two lovers going at it in his bed.

Aarav grabbed the bottle of coconut oil from where they'd abandoned it on the nightstand. "Are you telling me something?"

Cash hadn't really planned to be so blatant but, hey, he wasn't about to say no. He paused what he was doing to Sola to look over his shoulder and grin. "Never said I was subtle. Go for it."

Sola moaned. As he returned his attention to her slickening folds, she gripped his thighs on either side of her head. Good thing she had a firm hold because when Aarav spread his ass and his oiled fingers pressed against Cash's opening, he jerked. His cock slipped free of Sola's light suction and slapped her cheek.

She quickly recaptured him, encouraging him to reward her by introducing several of his fingers to her even as Aarav did the same to him. Aarav wised up and used his spare hand to cup Cash's balls, running his thumb along the incredibly sensitive spot where they dangled from the base of his cock and using the grip to keep Cash still.

Cash mimicked Aarav's penetration with his own fingers inside Sola, thrilled by how she hugged him with her velvety heat, smothering him even as he clenched around Aarav's thick digits.

It felt too amazing for him to do this for long. He didn't intend to end their sharing so soon by pumping his release down Sola's skilled throat. So he concentrated on flicking his tongue over her clit in the pattern she preferred, swirling it and sucking each time his fingers reached deep inside her. When her thighs began to quiver on either side of his face, he curled them, pressing against the front wall of her channel.

Sola didn't even try to resist. She allowed him to usher her into a powerful climax, secure in the knowledge that between him and Aarav, they had plenty more in store for her. When her cries spaced out and quieted, he lifted his head, nipping her thigh as she released him from her suckling lips with a slick pop.

Cash rolled, letting her rest on his torso instead of being crushed by him. The motion knocked Aarav's fingers from within him, which was for the best. Too much more of that delicious pressure and the occasional tap against his prostate was going to send him tumbling into orgasm before he was ready.

Truth was, he wanted something more than quick and simple gratification. He needed to be joined with both his lovers, whom he was surer day by day were also his soulmates.

"Aarav, give me a minute?" Cash asked, his breathing rough.

"I can do that." His voice was warm and liquid, his accent thicker than when he wasn't extremely turned on. Sola's sweet weight was lifted from him. Even though she was only gone for a few seconds, he missed her until Aarav laid her back into his arms, this time face to face.

She hummed and ground against him, rubbing her clit on the ridge of his cock.

"You want more?" Aarav asked her as he traced a line down her spine with three fingers.

"Damn straight." She nuzzled the crook of Cash's neck, then began to kiss and suck just below his ear. The sound he made was unintelligible, and yet they seemed to understand.

Aarav laughed and stepped between Cash's legs, which dangled off the end of the bed, his feet planted on the floor. With Sola clinging to him, her pussy was at the perfect height for Aarav. He fisted his cock and advanced, pressing into her in a single fluid stroke.

"Ah!" Sola cried out and shuddered in Cash's hold as if being joined with Aarav was enough to set off a massive aftershock in her. Hell, it probably was.

Aarav wrapped her hair around his hand and pulled her head back, exposing her neck to Cash, who took the opportunity to treat her to the same sweet torture she'd inflicted on him. Her pussy soaked his dick as she kept riding his length, while fucked by Aarav within her.

"Son of a bitch, you're hot," he murmured to Sola as she impaled herself on his dick and used Cash's to tease her clit on every pass.

"You both are." Cash admired them as they pleased themselves by pleasing each other.

Sola stared into his eyes as Aarav fucked her, ramping up the pace as the intensity of their connection spurred him to escalate their coming together. He pressed the flat of his hand to the small of Sola's back, arching her ass upward as he plunged inside her. The compression also trapped Cash's cock more solidly between them. If they weren't careful, simply kissing her as she unraveled over him was going to be enough to cause him to make a mess of both their six packs.

But no, not yet.

Cash gritted his teeth as Sola surrendered to the relentless shuttling of Aarav's cock within her. She flew, trusting him to keep her grounded as Aarav rode her through her second orgasm. Once Sola had calmed, the puffs of her breath buffeting his neck, Aarav withdrew with a strangled groan.

"I can't wait anymore." He ran his hand through the black waves of his hair, a sheen of perspiration covering his chest.

Cash helped Sola sit up. Straddling him, she grinned before flashing her wicked smile at Aarav over her shoulder. "This is never going to get old."

Cash was prepared to let Aarav fuck him as he waited for Sola to recover, but he should have known better. She wasn't the kind of woman to take breaks. She was a sprinter, a force of nature, and she hadn't yet had her fill of them.

Sola raised up enough to lift his cock and aim it toward her core. She fit them together and sheathed his cock as she lowered herself once more.

"Who wants me?" Aarav asked.

"I always do," Sola promised. "But today, I think Cash needs you more and he's plenty for me."

Her words had as much impact as the force of her pussy strangling his dick. Had he ever been enough for anyone? Certainly not his father.

But these two people, they loved him. Not in spite of his flaws or his quirks, but because of them.

Cash looked over Sola's shoulder to where Aarav had his hands on his hips and was likely practicing physics calculations of bullet trajectories in his brain to keep from erupting after Sola had wrung his dick so recently. "She's right. Fuck me, Aarav."

Sola sat up straight and reached behind her, hooking her hand around the back of his neck. She tipped her head back and kissed Aarav while he encircled Cash's ankles in an unbreakable grip and placed them on his powerful shoulders.

Cash's sharp inhale drew Sola's attention. She kneaded his chest, then leaned forward, which caused his cock to impale her fully. He hugged her tight as she worked over him, balancing out the slight discomfort of Aarav's fat cock stretching his ass open with the sensuous glide of her pussy over his shaft.

He felt stuffed, full of them and his emotions, which expanded exponentially every time they were joined together in some arrangement of their three bodies.

His favorite moments were these, where he couldn't possibly deny how good and how right they were together because of the way he instinctively responded to their every touch, kiss, and fuck.

Aarav and Sola moved in tandem, filling and smothering him with their heat. He prayed that Aarav had run out of restraint. Because Cash had stopped making excuses for why this couldn't be exactly as mind-blowing as he'd imagined and he didn't stand a chance of lasting when both of these incredible people shared this intimate moment with him.

Most of all, because they loved him as much as he loved them.

That thought alone nearly made him shoot deep inside Sola. He needed them to understand how they made him feel but elaborate pledges were beyond him right then. So he kept it simple. "I love you. Both of you."

"And I love you." Sola looked at both of them before Aarav also repeated the sentiment. His hips hitched and then he broke, going wild. He rode Cash as if he couldn't maintain his legendary composure for a single moment more.

How had anyone ever thought him cold? Aarav released every bit of his suppressed emotions, trusting Sola and Cash with the parts of him he'd never shared before, same as Cash was doing in return.

As his balls gathered and drew up tight to his body, Cash gripped Sola's hips, helping her move faster and farther over him. He fucked up into her even as Aarav chased him, his hips slapping Cash's ass as the three of them came together, permanently.

Sola led them into rapture, throwing her head back, her long hair brushing Cash's balls and the place where Aarav joined them together. He slid his hands up to her perfect tits and squeezed, anchoring her as she shattered. The undulation of her pussy drew him with her into an epic orgasm that was only made more magnificent by Aarav's thick cock tunneling in and out of his ass.

In a perfect chain reaction, Cash's pleasure spread to Aarav as Cash's muscles ratcheted on the base of Aarav's dick. Aarav cursed in his native language, somehow sounding even sexier than usual as he flooded Cash's ass.

Cash overflowed Sola's pussy. A thin white bead of his come seeped from her, sliding down his shaft as proof of his thorough satisfaction.

Aarav slumped over Sola, hugging her as he twitched, the last several waves of his climax passing through to Cash in spurts. They stayed connected—kissed and caressing, murmuring praise and promises—for as long as their bodies would allow.

And when Aarav finally softened enough to slip free of Cash's ass, he disappeared only briefly to clean himself up then brought a washcloth and tended to both Sola and Cash.

They'd curled up in the big bed together, cuddling as they soaked in the gratitude they had for the way they could make each other feel and the fact that they had survived this nightmare—more whole than ever before because they had found their missing pieces in each other.

It was around the time Cash thought he might doze off given the bone-deep serenity coursing through him and the sleepless hours he'd endured the previous two nights that an odd scraping noise from the other room caught his attention. "What's that?"

He might not have cared enough to investigate, but Aarav sat upright, then bolted into the kitchen.

Sola and Cash chased him, lurching to a stop when they realized Miss Nibbles had somehow gotten on the countertop and was helping herself to the salad Aarav had been in the middle of making when Sola knocked. She'd burrowed into the salad and was munching a carrot held in her adorable paws, looking up at them from the bowl like she'd found her own personal paradise.

They should have scolded her, but none of them bothered, especially not when they could relate.

Sola laughed, the sound lighter and easier than he'd ever heard from her before. She patted the bunny on the head and said, "You know, we have a friend, Mr. Prickles. I think the two of you might get along really well."

Cash had no idea what it was about this place that seemed to collect misfits and strays and turn them into the perfect network of friends and...family...but he knew he'd never been as lucky as the day they'd been sent to execute him and decided to make him one of their own instead. He hadn't exactly found his purpose yet, aside from adoring his two wonderful partners, but he was sure they would help him discover what he was meant for in addition to loving them.

For now, that was more than enough.

When Aarav asked their home automation system to play some music and started shaking his ass to a song laced with a strong beat overlaid with sitar, he knew they'd ended up exactly where they'd always been meant to be.

20

———————

Ace punched Liam in the shoulder as they left the gym. It was more of a love tap, but it felt so good to be able to have full use of his arm again with that damn cast off. "Thanks for staying late to work out with me. I didn't want to wait another day to get back at it."

"No problem. Can't have you getting stronger than me." Liam teased. They both knew no matter how many hours Ace put in at the gym rehabbing the arm he'd recently broken on a mission, he'd never bulk up to Liam's standards. The man was practically a walking mountain.

Not that Ace was complaining, and certainly didn't when they spent alone time in bed together, with Liam covering him, the weight of his muscles a warm comfort. They'd been partners at Shields for a few months now, but partners in life a whole lot longer.

Ace laughed at the man who was his roommate, and so much more, as they rounded the corner past the lobby of the Shields headquarters. Down the hall, before the elevators to the living quarters upstairs, was the command center and then the kitchen where they shared so many meals and fun times with the rest of their found family.

Coming to Shields had been one of the best decisions they'd ever made. Not only for their careers, but also for the stability of their relationship and the support system they'd found. Not to mention the sweet and sexy woman they'd both had their eyes on from the moment they'd been introduced to her. Ruby.

Figuring out how to approach her without ruining all those other amazing aspects of being a Shield, well...that was something they hadn't figured out yet.

"Did someone forget to turn the light off? Let me get it quick." Liam spotted the glow coming from beneath the command center door at the same time Ace did.

They turned long enough for him to pop it open. But instead of flicking the light off and continuing toward their apartment, a long, steamy shower together, and the massage of his arm Liam had promised—which would absolutely lead to massaging other parts of him, hopefully with Liam's mouth and cock—Liam froze. "Ruby? What are you doing?"

Ace went onto his tiptoes to peek over Liam's massive shoulder at the woman typing furiously from the gaming chair she'd insisted James buy for her. The thing looked like it belonged in a racecar. Considering her deft handling of the mega-computer in front of her, checking various screens in the bank of at least ten monitors arranged in an arc before her as her fingers flew over the keyboard and mouse, he figured it wasn't so different.

She could probably run the world from that thing.

Liam entered cautiously and Ace followed on his heels. Not wanting to startle her, he called, "Hey, earth to Ruby."

Still no response. It could have been because of the headset she was wearing, but more likely she was hyper-focused on whatever she was doing. In fact, he didn't even see her blink as they approached. When Liam tapped her shoulder, she screeched and whipped around so fast the cord on her headphones jerked her head back.

"Sorry!" Liam held his hands up, palms facing her. "It's late. Everything okay?"

Ace could already tell it wasn't. Her usually pale skin was ghost-white, her bright red hair seeming even more vibrant against her translucent complexion. Her pulse pounded in her neck and her eyes were wide and watery.

Ruby glanced away, back to her computer and tried to get rid of them. "Sure. Fine. Everything's peachy. Sorry, guys, but I need to concentrate right now."

"On what?" Liam wasn't about to leave her any more than Ace was. Something wasn't right.

Ruby never panicked. She was always flippant, and a bit dismissive. Never so serious and certainly not downright fucking scared. Whatever she was doing was bad news.

"I'm not sure..." she muttered as she hit ten-thousand different keys, staring at a string of characters flying by that might as well have been Chinese for all he could understand them. "I was mining some blockchain because House of Goblins is releasing an NFT I wanted to get in on."

Ace whipped his gaze to Liam, who shrugged. He heard the words she was saying, but they weren't making sense in his brain. His mind translated it as *computer stuff, womp womp womp womp womp.*

"What's blockchain?" Liam asked.

"It's the foundation for cryptocurrencies," Ruby answered without giving them an ounce of her attention.

"And NFT stands for...?" Ace wondered.

"Non-fungible token." More clattering of keys. "It's like digital art. Potentially very valuable if you get in early and sell to the right person."

"Damn, Ruby. You're so fucking smart you make me feel like I've got rocks for brains." Liam seemed suitably impressed, and so was Ace. Ruby also made him feel like he had a rock for a cock, but that was a whole other discussion. She was clearly not interested in them enough to even turn around and look at them or she would have seen exactly how into her they were.

"I'm not. I'm a fucking idiot. Because while that was running, I was digging around on the creators to see what I could find out and decide if this was going to be a good investment, which is a little bit of a no-no." Ruby rocked as she spoke, as if trying to calm herself down, but it didn't seem to be working.

"I see." Ace had done plenty of dumb things in his life, including rebellious ones. He liked that side of Ruby as much as her adorable nerd side and her loyal friend side and of course her hot geek girl side.

"You pissed someone off?" Liam grew more serious then, crouching on one side of her. "Are you in trouble?"

"So. Much. Trouble." Ruby gnawed on her lower lip. "Look. You should go. Forget you saw me in here and that we had this conversation."

"Like fucking hell we will." Ace mirrored Liam, settling in for the long haul. But it was hard to figure out how to fight a computer or protect her from another keyboard warrior, who knew where in the world.

"I just wanted to be sure about what I was seeing."

Ruby's voice quaked. "Before I brought this up to Jordan or JRad." JRad was her mentor and a computer whiz who worked for the Men in Blue at the OSPD.

"What did you uncover?" Liam asked gently.

"This shouldn't be possible." Ruby's eyes were huge as she stared at the monitors. "Someone is scamming the system. These aren't real sequences. It's like they're printing fake money. Billions and billions of dollars' worth of it. If this came out, it could undermine all cryptocurrencies and the entire market could collapse. It would be a global disaster."

Just then, she went ramrod straight as if someone had electrocuted her through her keyboard. Instead of the endless string of symbols flying past, her screen turned into one single image displayed across all the monitors.

An animated mask popped onto the screen and spoke in an eerie, digitally altered voice. "You're going to leave now. And consider yourself lucky that all we've taken for bothering us is your life savings. Next, we come for you. Don't think those assholes you work with can protect you either. We see everything. We know everything. And we'll be watching you."

Ruby recoiled, drawing her bare feet up onto the seat of the chair and flinging her arms around her legs. When she laid her head on her knees and buried her face, she began to sob.

Liam looked across her to Ace as panic and terror constricted his pupils. He went into the same mode he did on an assignment, turning into a warrior who would no doubt annihilate anyone who dared to hurt Ruby, the same way he'd—without hesitation—put a bullet in the brain of the bastard who'd broken Ace's arm and would have done a lot worse, too.

Both of them looked at each other, utterly helpless and with no idea of how to fix whatever shitstorm Ruby had stirred up. But they were going to have to figure it out.

To FIND out what it takes to bring Ruby, Ace, and Liam together, read their story, Broken.

If you'd like to start at the very beginning of the Powertools world and read more about James and his partners, you can download a discounted boxset of the first six books HERE.

Yes, I know it says complete series but I wrote a seventh book more recently and haven't gotten around to updating the boxset yet, sorry!

You can find the seventh Powertools book, More the Merrier, HERE.

They are also featured in four books in the Powertools: The Original Crew Returns series starting with Screwed HERE

To read more about the Hot Rides gang—where you'll find Jordan, Wren, and Kason's full story—start with Quinn, Trevon, and Devra's book, Wild Ride, click HERE.

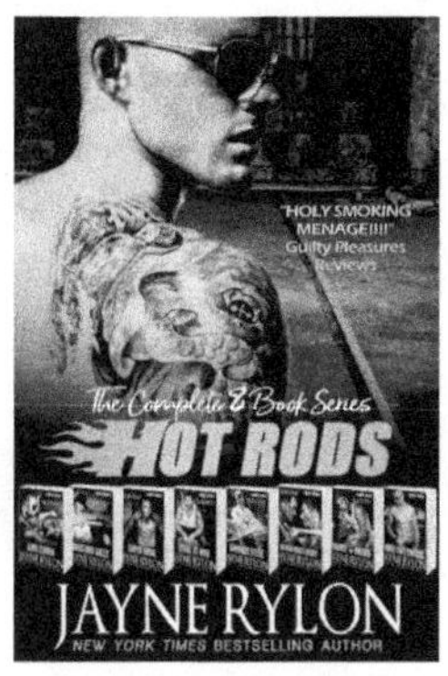

If you missed out on the Powertools: Hot Rods series, you can buy all eight books in a discounted single-volume boxset by clicking HERE.

Did you know Jayne brought the original Powertools crew back for four more books? Click HERE to get caught up.

CLAIM A $5 GIFT CERTIFICATE

Jayne is so sure you will love her books, she'd like you to try any one of your choosing for free. Claim your $5 gift certificate by signing up for her newsletter. You'll also learn about freebies, new releases, extras, appearances, and more!

www.jaynerylon.com/newsletter

WHAT WAS YOUR FAVORITE PART?

Did you enjoy this book? If so, please leave a review and tell your friends about it. Word of mouth and online reviews are immensely helpful and greatly appreciated.

JAYNE'S SHOP

Check out Jayne's online shop for autographed print books, direct download ebooks, reading-themed apparel up to size 5XL, mugs, tote bags, notebooks, Mr. Rylon's wood (you'll have to see it for yourself!) and more. www.jaynerylon.com/shop

LISTEN UP!

The majority of Jayne's books are also available in audio format on Audible, Amazon and iTunes.

ABOUT THE AUTHOR

Jayne Rylon is a New York Times and USA Today bestselling author, who has sold more than two million copies of her books. She has received numerous industry awards including the Romantic Times Reviewers' Choice Award for Best Indie Erotic Romance and the Swirl Award, which recognizes excellence in diverse romance. She is an Honor Roll member of the Romance Writers of America. Her stories used to begin as daydreams in seemingly endless business meetings, but now she is a full time author, who employs the skills she learned from her straight-laced corporate existence in the business of writing. She lives in Ohio with her husband, the infamous Mr. Rylon, and kittens they foster for a rescue organization. When she can escape her purple office, she loves to travel the world, avoid speeding tickets in her beloved Sky, SCUBA dive, and–of course–read.

Jayne Loves To Hear From Readers
www.jaynerylon.com
contact@jaynerylon.com
PO Box 10, Pickerington, OH 43147

facebook.com/jaynerylon

twitter.com/JayneRylon

instagram.com/jaynerylon

youtube.com/jaynerylonbooks

bookbub.com/profile/jayne-rylon

amazon.com/author/jaynerylon

ALSO BY JAYNE RYLON

4-EVER

A New Adult Reverse Harem Series

4-Ever Theirs

4-Ever Mine

EVER AFTER DUET

Reverse Harem Featuring Characters From The 4-Ever Series

Fourplay

Fourkeeps

EVER & ALWAYS DUET

Reverse Harem Featuring Characters from the 4-Ever and Ever After Duets

Four Money

Four Love

POWERTOOLS: THE ORIGINAL CREW

Five Guys Who Get It On With Each Other & One Girl. Enough Said?

Kate's Crew

Morgan's Surprise

Kayla's Gift

Devon's Pair

Nailed to the Wall

Hammer it Home

More the Merrier *NEW*

POWERTOOLS: HOT RODS

Powertools Spin Off. Keep up with the Crew plus...

Seven Guys & One Girl. Enough Said?

King Cobra

Mustang Sally

Super Nova

Rebel on the Run

Swinger Style

Barracuda's Heart

Touch of Amber

Long Time Coming

POWERTOOLS: HOT RIDES

Powertools and Hot Rods Spin Off.

Menage and Motorcycles

Wild Ride

Slow Ride

Hard Ride

Joy Ride

Rough Ride

POWERTOOLS: RETURN OF THE CREW

The original crew is back with more steamy menage stories!

Screwed

Drilled

Grind

Pound

POWERTOOLS: THE SHIELDS

Do-gooder Polyamorous Assassins in MMF Menages

Found

Lost

Brazen

Broken

Claimed

Shared

MEN IN BLUE

Hot Cops Save Women In Danger

Night is Darkest

Razor's Edge

Mistress's Master

Spread Your Wings

Wounded Hearts

Bound For You

DIVEMASTERS

Sexy SCUBA Instructors By Day, Doms On A Mega-Yacht By Night

Going Down

Going Deep

Going Hard

STANDALONE

Menage

Middleman

Nice & Naughty

Contemporary

Where There's Smoke

Report For Booty

COMPASS BROTHERS

Modern Western Family Drama Plus Lots Of Steamy Sex

Northern Exposure

Southern Comfort

Eastern Ambitions

Western Ties

COMPASS GIRLS

Daughters Of The Compass Brothers Drive Their Dads Crazy And Fall In Love

Winter's Thaw

Hope Springs

Summer Fling

Falling Softly

COMPASS BOYS

Sons Of The Compass Brothers Fall In Love

Heaven on Earth

Into the Fire

Still Waters

Light as Air

PLAY DOCTOR

Naughty Sexual Psychology Experiments Anyone?

Dream Machine

Healing Touch

RED LIGHT

A Hooker Who Loves Her Job

Complete Red Light Series Boxset

FREE - Through My Window - FREE

Star

Can't Buy Love

Free For All

PICK YOUR PLEASURES

Choose Your Own Adventure Romances!

Pick Your Pleasure

Pick Your Pleasure 2

RACING FOR LOVE

MMF Menages With Race-Car Driver Heroes

Complete Series Boxset

Driven

Shifting Gears

PARANORMALS

Vampires, Witches, And A Man Trapped In A Painting

Paranormal Double Pack Boxset

Picture Perfect

Reborn

PENTHOUSE PLEASURES

Naughty Manhattanite Neighbors Find Kinky Love

Taboo

Kinky

Sinner

Mentor

ROAMING WITH THE RYLONS

Non-fiction Travelogues about Jayne & Mr. Rylon's Adventures

Australia and New Zealand

www.ingramcontent.com/pod-product-compliance
Lightning Source LLC
Chambersburg PA
CBHW070926190726
48292CB00004B/1118